THE SLEEPING BEAUTY

THE OBSIDIAN SPINDLE SAGA
BOOK ONE

RUSSELL NOHELTY

SPECIAL THANKS

Adriane Ruzak, Amanda Jackson, Angela, Anthony Bachman, Caledonia, Caspar Williams, Celeste and Bryan Cornish, Chad Bowden, Chris Call, Chris Meeson, Christopher C Epping, Christopher Prew, CJ Ives Lopez, Daniel Biittner, Daniel Groves, Dave Baxter, Dave Goldberg, David Chamberlain, David Drummond, David Straube, Desiree Duffy, DJ Inzeo, Ed S, Edward Nycz Jr., Emerson Kasak, Erin Congdon, Gabriella Farmer, Gary Phillips, Hannah Long, Hollie Buchanan II, Jeff Lewis, Jennifer & Charlie Geer, John C. Heller, Johnny Britt, Jon Tugan, Joshua Bowers, Joshua Pantalleresco, Juli, Kimberly Herout, Larry Gilman, Lincoln City Archery, Lisa Homolka, Lisa Lyons, Matthew Johnson, Maxi Organ, Melissa Showers, Michael Kingston, Michael Perler, Mike Jones, Monkey King Comics, Nic Nelson, Nick Smith, Paul Rose Jr., Per Stalby, Rachel Adams, Rhel ná DecVandé, Richard A Williams, Rob MacAndrew, Rowan, S.A. McClure, Salvatore Puma, Scott Kilburn, Stephen Ballentine, Steven "Waffles" Lane, Taiga Char, Talinda Willard (everfai), Victoria Nohelty, and Walter Weiss

The Sleeping Beauty
Book 1 of the Obsidian Spindle Saga

By:
Russell Nohelty

Edited by:
Leah Lederman

Proofread by:
Katrina Roets

Cover by:
JV Arts

Formatting by:
Turbo Kitten Industries

PROLOGUE
CHELLE

I knew it was going to be a bad day when I stepped out of the house with two different shoes on my feet. I did not think it would be so bad as to end with me strung upside down on a meat hook in the back of an abandoned warehouse.

"Tell me where the gold is!" a gap-toothed, bald man hissed.

I was surprised they didn't put a cloth bag over my head. Most monster hunters were superstitious, and they believed the old wives' tale that gorgons could turn people into stone with just a look. We can't.

"Does it look like I have any gold?" I asked. "Both of my shoes have holes in them."

Blood dripped from the corner of my mouth onto the floor. Idiots were always surprised that my blood ran red, but I was only half-gorgon after all. The human part of me didn't give me the strength necessary to break through steel and take my captors out. If I was full gorgon, I would have already ripped them in half.

A squirrelly, lanky man with bad teeth and a pasty complexion knelt next to me, his knee barely missing the pool of blood gathering on the floor. The harem of snakes growing from my head snapped at him, but my abductor remained just out of their reach.

"Look here, little one. We been doing this long enough that we can smell a gorgon anywhere, and we know one thing. Where there's gorgon, there's gold. It's that simple."

I turned my eyes to the feckless twerp and spat blood all over him. The man scurried away, apparently worried my blood might burn him like hydrochloric acid. Unfortunately, that wasn't one of the gifts bestowed upon me by my mother's DNA.

"There is no gold!" I shouted. "Trust me, if there were, I wouldn't be living out of my car."

The fat, bald man walked forward and grabbed me around the waist. The tendril of snakes growing from my head hissed at him, and he growled back at them. Unfortunately, my snakes were not poisonous, just a nuisance, so I couldn't use them to kill our captors.

He smiled at me. In the battle to capture me, I had kicked out his front teeth, and I took great satisfaction in seeing the gap where his teeth should have been.

"We have all night, little one."

He turned me around and around until the chain kinked and wouldn't go another rotation. Then he let me go. I swung violently around a dozen or more times before I came to a stop in the other direction, and then spun back again, repeating that process again and again until the chain finally settled down and the Twinkie that was my lunch hurled out and splattered on the ground, mixing with the blood beneath me.

"Soon enough all the blood that's left in your body is gonna pool to your brain and your eyes will pop outta your head from the pressure."

"Actually," I said, trying to hold in what remained of the lunch in my stomach, "that wouldn't really happen. It's a myth."

The lanky man stepped forward. "Well, then how come we seen it with our own eyes?"

I cocked my head toward him. "Because you're liars. All of you are liars. Every monster hunter I've ever met has been nothing more than a lying, sniveling coward, who couldn't find a self-respecting job, so they decided to fill the hole in their souls by picking on my kind."

"Well," the bald one said, "at least you admit you're a monster. That's progress."

"I'm not ashamed of what I am. I'm just trying to get by. I'm ashamed for you, though. Because you're a pussy."

Without saying another word, the bald man raised his boot and connected it with my face. My head snapped back, and I passed out.

When I woke up, I was alone. I don't know why people always left unconscious people unguarded. Maybe they saw it in the movies, or maybe they were just stupid enough to believe I was helpless.

I may not have gotten all my mother's powers, but she taught me a thing or two about using magic. The chains that bound me were carved with runes and enchanted to make sure I couldn't cast a spell to unfurl them, but they had made the critical error of not wiping up the blood that dripped from my nose.

I closed my eyes. "*Sanguinem glacies adstricta. Mihi reserare*"

Latin was the best language for spells. They were never as powerful in any other language, so I forced myself to learn the minimum amount of Latin required to make them work. None of the Latin I took in high school stuck, which meant I resorted to using Google Translate once I worked everything else out about the spell. My grammar was horrible, but the spells were effective none the less. Somebody once told me that spell casting was half confidence, and at least in that aspect of being a mage, I got an A plus.

The blood on the ground coalesced into little needles and shot up toward the lock that bound my feet. The chains were exceptionally strong, but the weak point with all chains was the lock. A hundred blood needles shot into the metal lock, and in my mind's eye I saw them push inside the lock and liquify again.

"*Pruinae*," I whispered, and the blood turned to ice. I looked up and saw the lock turn to a bright blue. "*Praemium*."

The lock exploded into a million pieces and scattered throughout the dark warehouse. I struggled to loosen my chains, and eventually I wiggled free enough to emerge from my metal chrysalis and slam onto the ground.

"Not very much like a butterfly," I mumbled to myself, pulling off my black leather coat that was now stained with vomit and blood. "That's going to the cleaners."

"What's going on in here?" The bald man shouted as he shuffled across the warehouse. I could have run into the darkness and avoided a confrontation, but if I did, then they wouldn't learn anything. If I let them go, they would hunt me again. Or worse, they would hurt some other monster who couldn't defend themselves.

I wrapped the metal chain around my wrist and pulled it from the meat hook. When the bald man saw me, he went for his gun. I whipped the chain at him. The lanky man came up next to him, and I flung the chain at his face, smacking him across the cheek with it.

I rushed the men, roundhouse-kicking the fat one in the stomach and tying the chain around him. I squeezed it tight and pulled him to the floor. The skinny man swung at me, and I blocked it with my arm before wrapping him up with the other side of the chain and kicking the back of his knees, so he dropped to the ground. They both screamed when I yanked the chain tight.

"Don't eat us, please!" the fat one said.

"We won't say nothing," the other one squeaked. "We promise. Just let us go."

I smiled. "Wow. You really think the worst of me, don't you? That really is the lowest opinion of me I've ever heard. I'm not going to eat you, but I can't have you following me, either."

My eyes glowed yellow and I grabbed the faces of both men and turned them toward me. "Listen to me, closely."

"I don't wanna become stone!" the fat man said.

"I'm too young to die!" the skinny man added.

I dug my fingers into their cheeks. "OPEN YOUR EYES!"

They couldn't fight me any longer without passing out. Their eyes popped opened and started to glow in time with mine. "You will forget you ever found me. You will tell anybody who asked that the last you heard I was headed to Zimbabwe to find my ancestral home. When you regain your faculties, you will lose your taste for hunting monsters, and get menial jobs pushing papers in some government agency far away from here. Am I understood?"

"Yes, mistress," they both said in unison.

"Good." I pulled the chains from off them. I blinked, and my eyes turned back from yellow to their deep green. "Now, off you go."

The men turned to each other, confused. They didn't say a word. They just looked at each other, then to me, then to each other.

"I think you have some jobs to apply for, don't you?" I asked.

The fat man nodded. "Yeah, I think this monster hunting business has run its course, don't you?"

The skinny man looked dazed. "I think I'm ready to become a company man, get fat, and have a gaggle of kids."

"That sounds like a good plan, gentlemen. One final thing. If I ever see you again...I'll rip your throats out and eat them in front of you as you die gasping for air. Got it?"

"Got it," they replied in unison.

"Good. Now, have a great day."

I walked toward the door. Before I got there, I found the wig my abductors had taken from me. I had long ago learned to tame the snakes growing from my head with spells and draughts of sleeping potions, but I couldn't conceal them completely. Hence the wigs. If anybody else saw the snakes on my head and learned that monsters really existed, well, it wouldn't be good for anybody.

I ran my fingers through the tendrils of snakes flowing across my head, and they cooed at my touch. I grabbed the wig from the table and put it on before pulling the hood up from my sweatshirt. It would have to do until I could get to a bathroom and clean myself up.

CHAPTER 1
ROSE

Working nights sucked. I was so tired every day I was barely able to keep my eyes open during classes, let alone finish my assignments on time...but then again, it was best not to complain, especially about things I could do very little about. I drew the short straw in life, what with being birthed by unsupportive, poor, and uneducated parents that didn't trust higher education. If I wanted a degree, I had to suffer for it, and I really wanted a degree.

"No," I said, rubbing my temples as I tried not to sigh deeply into my headset. "You can't just put just any credit card number into the system and expect it to work."

The angry woman on the other end of the line had been badgering me for five minutes. "Why not?"

"Because that's fraud, ma'am."

"That's stupid. I want to speak to your supervisor!"

I sighed. "Gladly. Please hold."

I pressed the hold button on my receiver and typed in my supervisor's number. "Melody. I have a hot one for you."

I needed a break. I had been working since four pm and it was going on midnight. I still found it ridiculous that people cared about ordering vitamins at midnight, but in my time here at Tivarinex the one thing I had learned is that they cared about it deeply, so deeply they had a whole staff of late-night call center workers making sure their customers were happy. Their customers were the worst humans on the planet. Swamp monsters would have treated me better.

I shouldn't complain, though. They could have hired a call center in India to do the same job, but they kept it in America, and it wasn't their fault customers were the worst.

"Rose!" a curt voice snapped behind me.

I turned around to find my boss's boss, Christina, eyeing me. She did not look happy. Then again, she never looked happy. Probably because the way she painted on her eyebrows made her look perpetually pissed off at the world. Still, even for her, she looked particularly upset. "Yeah, boss?"

"I need to see you in my office. Now."

It wasn't much of an office, but Christina's cube was tucked away from the rest of the mayhem of the floor. It was quiet, or at least quieter than my cubicle, where I could hear every key typed and every word grumbled from the ten people around me.

"Do you remember Marvin Helfer?" Christina asked, sliding into her chair.

I shook my head. "No. It doesn't ring a bell, but then I talk to like a hundred people a day."

Christina harrumphed. "Well, you took his call five days ago, and let him put a card on file which turns out was stolen."

"Oh no," I said, bringing my hands to my mouth. "That's horrible. I'm so sorry."

"Yes," Christina said, flipping open a manila folder. "You have quite the history with fraudulent charges, don't you? We talked about it before, not two months ago."

"I know, but I've been better. I've been trying really hard. I just—"

"Not hard enough."

"I know but, like, at the end of the day isn't that up to our fraud department to figure this sort of thing out?"

"No, my dear," Christina said, slamming the folder on the desk. "It is your responsibility. It became your responsibility after the fifth time a fraudulent charge went through at your terminal in a single month."

"So what?" I braced for a scolding. My mother had the same look of disgust on her face right before she beat me with her belt. "Am I fired?"

"Hardly," Christina said. "If we fired you, then we would have to pay you severance, and then you would be stealing from this company for a second time."

"I'm not stealing. If anything, I'm negligent."

"You are definitely that."

"It's hard. With work, and school, and—"

"I don't care about your excuses. What I expect is professionalism from my employees, and in lieu of that, I expect them to keep their personal lives to themselves. Now, you will go back to your terminal and take a fraud seminar for the next three hours—unpaid —and I will be deducting this from your paycheck."

"What? You can't do that!"

She snickered. "I'm very sure that I can. Life will be very difficult for you from here on until you summarily quit or flame out, and I very much don't care which one it is."

I pushed myself up from my seat. I wanted so badly to quit, but I needed the job. There were very few night jobs that didn't involve scrubbing toilets.

"How much was the charge for? Twenty dollars?"

"Hardly. Seven hundred and thirty-four dollars, exactly."

"That's more than two weeks wages!" I shouted, digging my fingers into the back of my chair. "I have medicine I need to buy. It's literally life or death."

Christina twisted her mouth into a smile. "Then make sure not to make the same mistake again."

CHAPTER 2
CHELLE

Magic: The Gathering and *Charmed* made stupid people believe that gorgons could change shape. That's not how it worked, though. At least not for me. I haven't met every gorgon in the world, but none of those that I have met were shapeshifters. They were all just really good with makeup.

My mother taught me to be good with cosmetics. She hid my green complexion from the time I was a baby until her untimely death at the hands of the same type of monster hunters that stalked me endlessly. It was easier for me than it was for her, though. My father was dark skinned, so even if I didn't use foundation my green tinge was barely noticeable.

The plus side of being good with makeup was that it also allowed me to easily conceal a beating. It was helpful during middle school after my mom died, and in high school before my father abandoned me, but it became even more helpful when I started to run into monster hunters every couple of months.

The welt under my eye from my last encounter grew by the minute, and I feared that without ice I wouldn't be able to tamp it down in time for school the next day. I didn't need a bunch of my classmates asking questions. Hopefully, I could sit in the back of the classroom and have the reasonable expectation they would all think I was just hung over. They were a nosey bunch, no matter how much I tried to stay away from them.

The headache coursing down my neck felt like I had just woken up after a week-long bender. I needed to stop by the drug store to buy more concealer and a bag of ice. I was running low at home and hadn't been able to place an Amazon order yet. I had hoped to wait for some money to come in, but I guess I couldn't wait any more.

"Try this card," I heard from the register of the Walgreens when I walked toward the back of the store.

I turned to the counter to see Rose, my girlfriend, standing at the pharmacy checkout, her long, blonde hair pulled back in a greasy bun. She must have just gotten off work, because she still wore her black pantsuit and she hated that damn thing. She always pulled it off the moment she got home.

"Hey!" I ran up and hugged her from behind. "Funny meeting you here!"

"Baby!" She laughed and gave me a kiss. Her lips were soft, but she kissed with force enough to make sure I knew she was there. It wasn't ever a polite, obligatory kiss with Rose. It was always like the first time we'd kissed.

She pushed back my hood and saw the welt under my eye. "What happened to you?"

I pulled my hood back over my head. "Nothing."

"That's no—"

"I'm sorry, ma'am, but this card is declined, too." The pharmacist handed the card back to Rose.

"That's impossible. I just got it...please, is there anything you can do?"

He shook his head. "I'm sorry. You can go to the hospital if it's an emergency."

"Emergency!" Rose said through gritted teeth. "You realize if I don't get insulin I'll die, right? You get that, right? Is that an emergency to you?"

Rose was a diabetic, and it wasn't easy being diabetic and poor. Her parents cut her off from their insurance when we started dating, figuring it was better to have a dead daughter than a gay one, and every month it cost over seven hundred dollars to refill her medication.

"Babe!" I put my arm around her. "Calm down. It's not his fault."

She turned to me and buried her head in my shoulder. I could tell there was something else on her mind besides the insulin, but the fear of falling into a diabetic coma and dying was enough to put her in a bad state.

"Come on. Let's get some food in you. When was the last time you ate?"

"I don't need to eat. If anything, my levels are high. My heart is racing. I can hear it in my ears like the beating of that infernal Tell-Tale Heart."

"Well, I need to eat and not think about gothic horror for a minute. So, let's sit in a restaurant like two normal humans, calm down, figure this out, and you can check where your levels are."

She nodded. "Okay."

Joe's pizza was as awful as it was cheap, but it was cheap, and I didn't have money for anything else. I just needed calories, and Joe's was a greasy lard bomb. Two slices could keep me going for a whole day.

Rose pricked her finger as I wolfed down a piece of pepperoni pizza. She filled me in on her day at work after I finished telling her about my encounter with the monster hunters.

"Do you think they'll ever stop?" she said. "They seem to be coming more and more frequently with every passing month."

Rose was the first person outside of my family who I told the truth about who I was, and the only person I trusted, including my family, not to tell anybody about me. My father only learned the truth after my mother gave birth, and he tried to kill me a half dozen times in my first decade of life. When he ran out on me, I effectively became an orphan. The state tried to take me into their custody, but I ran away instead, and survived on the street until graduation.

"No. There will always be somebody that wants a quick buck."

Rose gave a snort. "That's funny. If you had any money, I wouldn't have to scrounge for insulin every month."

"And I wouldn't be living in your van. We would be living in a house, or at least a condo."

The insulin register beeped. Rose looked down at it. "It's really high. Like, fatally high. That's what I thought."

"How long since you've had a dose?"

"Two days. Some company approved me for another credit card, but it won't get here until tomorrow. I was hoping this paycheck would...I don't know what I'm going to do."

"Hey," I said, sliding my hand on top of hers. "We'll figure it out."

She looked up with me, her soft eyes tearing up. "I hope so. I don't know how long I have left until my body shuts down. I used up the GoFundMe money two months ago. I can't go back and beg for more. I can't even pay for your stupid pizza. You've given me every-thing you have. My parents—well, they aren't going to help."

The world was falling apart. We seemed to always be on the verge of nuclear war. Our leaders drove wedges between us, and it became a bigger chasm every day. We were caging children on our own borders, and cops were shooting black people just for existing. We couldn't even agree that black lives mattered, let alone that they should be allowed to live without being shot like animals. Still, of all the things wrong with the world, and even with it getting worse every day, nothing showed me this world was an unceasing cesspool of suck more than watching Rose dying and not having anywhere to turn for help.

"How is your Medicaid paperwork coming?"

"You know how it goes. They keep denying me for some reason or another. It's like the universe wants me to die."

I squeezed her hand. "I don't want you to die."

She chuckled and her face softened, looking into my eyes. Then she saw the fat welt swelling underneath them. "It's hard to believe with how terrible this night has been that it's only the second worst night between the two of us."

"It'll get better," I said, taking another bite.

"How do you know?" she said.

"Because I have to believe, Rose, or I might as well just kill myself right here."

CHAPTER 3
ROSE

It took Chelle eight months to tell me that she was a gorgon, but I suspected she was hiding something even on our first date. Her wig shifted while we were eating tacos and I swore I saw something move underneath her hair. I thought that it was just my eyes playing tricks on me at first, but then it shifted again, and the forked tongue of a snake flickered out her hairline. She excused herself to the bathroom, and when she came back her hair was matted to her head. The second date, I swore I heard something hissing under her hair, and on our third date I was sure that her eyes had flashed yellow, just for a second.

Still, she was sweet in a way that people hadn't ever been sweet to me in my whole life. My parents treated me like I was a burden, and my boyfriend in high school thought I was just a sex object who didn't have emotions, or thoughts of her own. He cheated on me repeatedly, but I kept going back. With how I was raised, I thought that's what it meant to be in love.

Chelle treated me differently. She wasn't my first girlfriend, but she was the one that saw through a hundred layers of broken and made me feel like a real person. I didn't know why or what, but there was something different about her.

She told me the truth on our eight-month anniversary, when she was pretty sure I would stay but not 100 percent certain. Her instincts were right about me, though. I've never wavered in my support of her.

Besides, I always kind of liked snakes, and the ones on Chelle's head were the cute garden variety, not the scary king cobra kind. They often nestled on my chest while Chelle slept.

"I'm tired," I said. "Can we go back?"

"Sure," Chelle said, squeezing my hand tighter.

Neither of us liked to be at home, but eventually we had no choice but to return to the van we shared. It wasn't much of a life, but we lived it together. Chelle's mother died when she was twelve, and her father abandoned her a couple years after. Even when he was there, he spent more time beating her than talking to her.

She ran away from foster care after her dad left and lived on the street until she graduated. She didn't have much to her name except the ratty clothes on her back and the crappy little Civic she brought to school. I didn't have much more, but I had saved up for a passenger van and converted it into a bedroom for the both of us.

Every morning I changed and showered at the gym and ate in the dining hall when I could scrounge together credits. Chelle did the same. Every once and a while friends took pity on us and transferred us credits. Other times, we starved. It wasn't much of a life, but everything would be better once we graduated, if I lasted that long.

"Hey, Greta!" I waved to a girl with long dreadlocks and a nose ring as we walked through the parking lot. We weren't the only ones who lived in the parking lot. There was a group of five or so cars that made us feel like a community. We all looked out for each other. Sometimes, I could bum a vial of insulin off somebody, even though I never had any to give.

"How are you feeling, Rose?" Greta said, smiling at me. Her nose ring glinted in the overhead light of the parking lot. She had dreadlocks that went down to her naval, and she pulled her long hair back with a bandana.

"Nauseous and hot, honestly."

"Come on," Chelle said, pushing on the small of my back. "You'll feel better in the morning."

Would I, though? Every night felt like my last night. I always feared that I would fall into a diabetic coma and never be able to wake up. I had to take insulin every day to live, but I hadn't taken any in two days. I didn't know when I could get another prescription. I was literally playing with my life.

"Lay down," Chelle said, sliding open the passenger door. "I'll get you some water."

I flopped into the mattress that had replaced the back seats. "No. Then I'll have to pee. I just want to sleep."

I didn't want to close my eyes, but I couldn't struggle to keep them open any longer. If I woke up again it would be a miracle. I had never felt as bad in my whole life. Of course, I couldn't say anything to Chelle, or she would worry. Maybe even take me to the hospital. I definitely couldn't afford that.

I just had to live with it and hope I would wake up again. If I didn't, at least all of this would be over.

CHAPTER 4
CHELLE

I brushed my teeth slowly in the library bathroom. The gym had better changing rooms, but the library was the only building on campus open twenty-four hours a day. Being alone with my thoughts in a quiet place never brought me solace. In the still darkness, my mind worked against me.

I thought back to my childhood, where I had to watch every move I made for fear of being beaten by my father. I looked for my mother for a month until they declared her dead. I don't know what affected me more, accepting that she was dead or making my first kill.

I spit out my toothpaste and wiped my mouth. My eye was nearly swollen shut now, and no amount of make-up could cover it up. I gingerly pressed the welt with my finger. The pain stiffened my whole body. In the heat of battle, the adrenaline stopped me from feeling any pain, but now in the quiet, pain was all I could feel: the welt under my eye, the bruises on my legs from the chains, and the throbbing pain in my shoulder. Compared to the rest of me, my migraine was a dull ache.

I left the library and hobbled back across the quad. By the time I got back to the car, all the lights in the parking lot were out. I slid open the door to Rose's van and hopped inside. Rose didn't move when I laid down next to her. I felt her chest to make sure she was breathing, and then drifted off to sleep myself. I had class in the morning, and I didn't look forward to it, or the residual pain I'd be sure to feel all day long. That was a problem for future Chelle. She would deal with that tomorrow. Now Chelle needed sleep.

I kicked the sliding door of the van closed and pressed the lock with my foot. Then, without another thought, I drifted off to sleep.

CHAPTER 5
ROSE

I woke up.

I actually woke up.

I felt horrible, but I woke up.

I gently rolled Chelle off me and crawled toward the door. Her wig tilted as she turned over, and her snakes popped open their eyes and cooed at me. I don't know how she was able to keep her secret for so long. She was miserable at disguises and subterfuge, but I was glad she shared it with me. It actually made me feel silly that I hadn't figured it out sooner. I quietly opened the door to the van and stumbled outside. I had to be careful that nobody saw Chelle in her natural state.

"Morning, Rose."

I turned to see Jamil, another one of my classmates living in her car. She had a big smile and was carrying a towel under her arm. We were headed to the same place. The gym opened at six, and we both needed a shower before class.

"How did you sleep?" I asked, opening the passenger's side door and pulling out my towel. I looked back to see Chelle still sleeping sweetly. It was difficult to believe she did anything sweetly, but she was a very peaceful sleeper, especially after a fight.

"You know, the El Camino isn't as nice as the camper, but I make do."

I followed her toward the sidewalk. "I'm telling you, a camper is where it's at. I converted this thing first semester and it's the best decision I ever made."

Jamil leaned in. "Don't let Chelle hear you say it."

"Hear me?" I chuckled. "She'd agree with me. Why do you think she's been with me so long? Her old jalopy can't compete."

"I'm gonna ask her, you watch." Jamil opened the door to the gym.

"Do it. I would love to know what she says."

The quick shower did little to alleviate my mood, or the sickness bubbling up in my stomach. By the time I turned the knob on the hot water, I could barely stand. I tried to lift my leg to dry it off, but I ended up stumbling back into the shower.

I sat down on one of the toilets to catch my breath, and after a couple of minutes the room stopped spinning. I was able to finish drying myself and put on my clothes, but when I got to the sink to brush my hair, a fire shot up through my stomach. I tried to catch myself on the counter, but my hands couldn't catch hold, and I fell onto the linoleum.

I pushed myself up to my knees. The room spun again, then everything went blurry. I fell into darkness.

CHAPTER 6
CHELLE

I woke up groggy and in a lot of pain from my fight the previous night. I popped two aspirin, and then two more, before stuffing the bottle in my backpack. I was glad Rose was feeling well enough to leave the van and venture out onto campus before me, but part of me had hoped she would be next to me when I got up. She had not been healthy for a long time, and it often took all her effort just to roll out of bed and get to class. Sometimes, she couldn't even do that, so I found myself taking notes in some of her classes, most of which I didn't understand.

I felt one of the snakes on my head yawn and looking in the mirror I saw it was Albert, the longest and most animated of my brood.

"Good morning, Albie," I said with a smile. I pulled a jar of dead crickets from behind the bed and fed him one. That got the other five snakes on my head excited, and I spent the next five minutes satiating them until they were pleasantly stuffed and settled back down on my head to nap again.

I stared at myself in the mirror for a full five minutes after that, watching the snakes sleep, and wondering how Rose could have fallen in love with such a hideous creature. I shook off the thought. I didn't have much time for it. I had an early class and needed to shower before it.

I pushed myself up, every bone and muscle creaking in my body as I did, donned one of my wigs, and a shower cap, then headed toward the gym, where I could ride the stationary bike for half an hour to warm up my muscles before hopping in the shower.

When I got there, a crowd had gathered. Flashing ambulance lights shone against the gym. Something was wrong, and my stomach immediately dropped. Then I saw Jamil, in the crowd, her thin hands clasped tightly against her mouth, and my gut dropped into my knees.

"Jamil," I said walking up to her, "what's going on?"

Jamil turned to me, tears in her eyes. "It's Rose. I found her... I don't know what happened, but..."

I didn't need to hear the rest. The doors swung open to the gym, and two EMTs were pushing Rose out on a cart. She was hooked up to an oxygen tank and looked barely alive, her skin a sickly and pale shade of death.

"Rose!" I said, rushing forward through the crowd. "Rose!"

Jamil pulled me back. "You can't do anything for her now. Come on. I'll take you to the hospital."

My mind blank, I let Jamil guide me back to her car. If anything happened to Rose, I didn't know what I would do. I didn't know how I would live in a world without her.

"She'll be okay," Jamil said, opening the passenger's door to her car. "She's a fighter."

I wanted to believe her, but I didn't, or I couldn't. Either way, I broke down crying.

CHAPTER 7
ROSE

I was falling.

Why was I falling?

Where was I?

Why couldn't I see anything?

What was happening?

I

Didn't

Like

This

Feeling.

Not

At

All.

Please make it stop.

CHAPTER 8
CHELLE

My head was clouded in a nervous fog the whole way to the hospital. I always knew in the back of my mind it was a possibility something would happen to Rose because of her diabetes, but I never actually put much stock in it. After all, we were young, and even though I was constantly being hunted, I would be lying if I didn't think we were a little invincible. Crappy things happened to us, but we always survived even if we didn't thrive.

Now, it wasn't so certain whether Rose would be okay. Bad things were supposed to happen to me, not her. She had already been through so much. I was supposed to handle enough bad things for the both of us.

Saint Ignatius Hospital was three miles from campus, but it felt like a million. When we finally arrived, I hopped out of the car and rushed toward the sliding glass doors before Jamil had even put it in park.

"Where is she?" I said, running into the hospital and up to the front desk.

"I don't know who you're talking about," the receptionist said with a thick layer of attitude. "There are like, two thousand people in this hospital."

"Rose. Rose Briar. She was brought here in an ambulance not long ago."

"If that's true, you're going to have to wait until she gets seen by the doctor before you can see her."

"I'm her emergency contact."

"Are you her sister? Mother? Father? Grandmother?"

"No," I said.

"Are you two married?"

I shook my head, deflated. "No."

The woman pointed her long, press-on fingernail toward the stiff blue seats behind me and sighed loudly. "Then, you're going to have to sit down and wait until visiting hours. Try to get in contact with her parents. They're the only ones who can see her now."

"She hates her parents."

"Then, I'm afraid she's on her own."

"That's not a very good answer."

"Well, it's the only one I got."

I stormed away from the counter and back toward Jamil, who had just entered the hospital. "Can I use your phone?"

I didn't have a cell phone. Even with burners, monster hunters kept tracking me down when I had one, so it was safer to rely on the kindness of strangers when the need arose, or in this case, the kindness of a friend.

Jamil pulled out the phone from her gold purse. "Of course. Who are you calling?"

"The Devil and her husband."

Rose's parents lived over an hour away from us. I expected them to tell me to piss off, but they sounded legitimately concerned, and were in their car before I was off the phone with them. Rose's parents weren't evil people, just bad ones. They completely disavowed their only daughter when she told them she was gay, and the sting hit double when Rose revealed she was dating a black woman.

She didn't tell them I was also half-Gorgon, but just being black was enough to make me a monster in their eyes.

"Where is she?" Rose's mom said, barreling through the door. Well, waddling was more like it. She was not the paragon of health, nor was her pock-faced husband. They both ate too much fast food, exercised too little, and smoked a carton a week, which made them wheeze and gasp with every step they took.

"She's—" I started, but her mother just blew past me.

"I'm not talking to you."

Rose's father sidled up to the reception desk. "I got a call that my daughter was in the hospital here. Her name is Rose Alice Briar."

"And you're her father?" the receptionist said.

He nodded. "That's right. I have ID to prove it if you need—"

"No. I believe you. I told her to call you," she said, pointing at me.

"Don't believe a word she tells you," Rose's mom said. "She's a liar and a home wrecker."

"I didn't wreck your home. You did that yourself." I snarled back at her.

Rose's mother clomped up to me. "Look at what you've done! Because of you, my daughter couldn't call her mother for help. She ended up here. Who knows what will happen to her now?"

I took a step forward. "Imagine what would have happened if you didn't kick her out and force her to be on her own just for loving who she loved."

"My daughter will never love a ni—"

"Katie!" Rose's father said. "She's not worth it. Come on. They said we can see her."

Rose's father handed her mother an ID badge and they turned toward the door. "She better be okay. Otherwise, we're gonna sue."

"Please," I said. "Please let me come."

Rose's father snarled at me. "Haven't you done enough?"

They walked through a sliding door that the receptionist pressed open for them and it closed behind their fat butts. The receptionist looked at me, doe-eyed, as if she finally found her heart. Tears welled in her eyes before she turned away from me. God forbid she show a bit of emotion.

"Thanks a lot. All I wanted was to see the person I love. Now you've left her with them."

The receptionist shook her head sadly. "I'm just doing what I'm told. Rules are rules."

"I'm sure they are."

I started to walk away, but the receptionist called behind me. "She's in a coma. They don't know when she'll wake up, or if she'll wake up."

Tears welled in my eyes. "Why did you tell me that?"

"I thought you should know. Clearly, you're somebody that loves her. Of course, if you tell anybody I said something, I'll deny it."

Jamil placed her hand on my shoulder. "Come on. There are other ways to help Rose."

I turned to her. "How?"

"I know a guy," Jamil smiled at me. "He'll be a lot more use to us than her parents."

"I should stay here. What if they—"

She squeezed my shoulder tight. "They won't, and she won't. Not unless we go now."

CHAPTER 9
CHELLE

"Can I say something to you without you getting offended?" Jamil said as she drove back toward school.

"No," I replied. "The answer to that has never been yes ever in the history of the world, but now you have to tell me, and deal with me being offended."

Jamil laughed. "Fine. I don't mean this to be offensive, but it probably will be."

"Just get on with it."

"You are really bad at hiding it."

"Hiding what?"

Jamil snickered. "Come on. Your makeup looks like it was done by a child, and there's a green tinge on your arms, legs, and neck. Do you even use concealer on the rest of your body?"

"I...I don't know what you're talking about," I said.

Jamil smiled, and then snapped her fingers. Instantly, she was the color of wood, and the texture of it as well. Her eyes were green, and her ears were pointed. "I'm very good at concealing myself."

"What are you?" I said, skittering back against the door.

"A dryad."

"A wood nymph?"

"I don't like the term 'nymph'," Jamil chuckled. "It implies I'm small and whimsical, and, as you can see, I'm neither of those things. Now, I'm going to turn back into my human form. Otherwise, everyone who drives past us will freak out."

Jamil snapped her fingers again, and she turned back into a human. In many ways, she was more human than I'd ever been.

"How did you do that?"

"See this amulet around my neck?" Jamil pulled a golden chain hidden under her shirt. A red ruby shone in the middle of it. "My friend sells them. He sells all sorts of magical stuff out of his dorm room. That's why we're going to see him. He knows more about magic than anybody I know."

"And your friend is—"

"He's a vampire. Don't make it a big thing. He hates humanity, but he fears death too much to end it all. He's kind of a bummer, but he's nice enough."

I sighed. "How long have you known about me?"

"Literally as long as I've known you. I mean, it took me a day or so to figure out you were a gorgon, but the monster part, that was almost instantaneous. You literally reek of monster. Probably why you're so easy to find."

"Hey!"

"What? I go to the same school as you and I haven't been found by monster hunters, literally ever. Meanwhile, you're like a homing beacon to them. How many times have they tracked you down? By my count it's twelve, but a couple of those black eyes could've been from bar fights, I guess."

"No, they were all monster hunters." I crossed my arms in a snit, but I couldn't deny she was right. "You know, I am offended by that."

"That doesn't make it any less true."

"I know. That makes me even more offended."

Waverly Hall was on the far end of campus closest to the woods, which gave it shade all throughout the day. It was the perfect place to conceal a vampire.

Jamil knocked loudly on the dorm room door after we'd snaked through the hallways. I didn't spend much time inside the dorms unless there was a party, and every time I did, I couldn't get over the stink of stale beer and moldy bread.

"Teddy is an interesting cat," Jamil said. "Don't look him directly in the eyes."

"Why?"

"Trust me."

"What do you want?" a shrill voice called from behind the door. "I'm takin' a nap. It's the middle of the day."

"I know, Teddy, but I have somebody here...she really needs to see you."

"Christ, is that Jam?"

Jamil nodded. "Yeah, it is."

"Well, why didn't you say so you beautiful ole dryad, you?"

"He knows?" I asked.

"He guessed, just like I guessed with you. Admittedly, I haven't always been this good at concealing myself."

Teddy swung open the door. He was rail thin, wearing nothing but a black kimono adorned with red and black flowers. He smoked a cigarette even though there were "no smoking" signs everywhere.

"You beautiful bastard," Teddy said, wrapping Jamil up in a big hug. He cocked his head when he saw me. "Who are you?"

I immediately understood why Jamil said not to make eye contact. Teddy's eyes were bright red, and not because they were bloodshot. His pupils were a dark burgundy, with bright red veins spidering off around them, drowning out the white.

"Oops," Teddy said. "Sorry, love." He pulled a pair of sunglasses from the pocket of his kimono and put them on. "Better?"

"It's fine," I replied. "I don't mind."

"Well, that's good. Most people do."

"I'm not most people. Besides, I have my own secrets."

Teddy leaned in and took a long whiff of me. "You being a gorgon's not much of a secret, you know?"

"Shhh," I said. "Somebody will hear."

"Who?" Teddy looked up and down the hall with melodramatic flourish. "I rented out all the rooms on this floor for privacy. You could actually kill a person here and nobody would be the wiser. Trust me. I've tested it."

"That seems expensive."

Teddy stretched his arms over his head. "Well, it's not really about the money. I just wanted a bit of the college experience. Without all the people bugging me, of course. I might look like a kid, but I'm four hundred years old, and I can't deal with hearing you children drone on about your problems."

"Well, I'm eighteen and I can't either."

"Then we've got that in common, love." Teddy smiled. "Thus, the privacy."

"That actually sounds...nice."

"I know. Come on, then. How can I help you?"

Teddy led us into his dorm room. There was a luxurious king bed against the wall. The four posts surrounding it were painted black to match the sheets and the rest of the decor. The windows were covered with black bags and tape. Glow-in-the-dark paintings of skulls and beautiful women lined the walls and gave off the only light in the room.

"Hrm..." I said.

"You were expecting to see a coffin, ay?" Teddy asked.

"I mean, that's what I've seen in movies."

"I haven't used a coffin in a hundred years. At least not since mattresses stopped being made of hay." Teddy flopped onto his bed. "Now, I know you're not here to talk about decorating, so get on with it."

Jamil closed the door. "Our friend is in a coma. We need to wake her up."

Teddy sat up. "Well, that's tricky isn't it? I mean, you can't just shake somebody awake when they're in a coma."

"I thought there might be some kind of spell or something," Jamil said.

Teddy smiled, exposing his jagged, sharp teeth. "There's a potion for most things, as you know. Unfortunately, comas are tricky business. How long has she been gone?"

"Since this morning," Jamil said. "I walked her to the gym about six am."

"Ooh, that's a long time. Wish you came to me earlier. There's not much I can do for her. You need more powerful magic than I've got here."

"Then what good are you?" I snarled, but immediately calmed down when Teddy gave me a disgusted expression. "I'm sorry. I'm just..."

"A bit emotional?" Teddy asked. His face softened. "That's understandable. Honestly, I wouldn't think much of you if you weren't."

"I just hate waiting and feeling helpless."

Teddy stood up. "I didn't say there was nothing you could do. It's just a little more complicated than what I can provide is all." Teddy shuffled over to his closet and began to rifle around in the menagerie of trash piled up inside of it. "There are a couple ways people wake up from a coma. Most of them are pretty dull. They involve no sort of magic or whimsy whatsoever. However, they are also nearly completely dependent on luck, no matter how much science tells you otherwise. I assume you're not a very lucky thing though, are you?"

I shook my head. "Neither of us are."

Teddy pulled out a framed poster from the back of his closet. "Then you need to visit the Obsidian Spindle."

"The what?" Jamil asked.

Teddy turned the poster toward us. The image glowed green, depicting a tall, sinewy tower, gnarled and dark, sitting on a cliff above a sea. The long bridge leading to it was guarded by a monstrous, roaring hydra, bound with a long, metal chain.

"The Obsidian Spindle is what controls fate. It's weaved by the three sisters, and they're the only ones who can wake somebody up from a coma, but only if you can find them."

I frowned, taking this all in. "Where...are they?"

Teddy smiled. "They're bound to the Dream Realm, caught between reality and myth."

I pursed my lips and nodded sarcastically. "All right, that's funny. You got me. I totally bought into your bullshit for a minute, but seriously. How can I wake her up?"

"I don't joke...not never." He gave Jamil a deadpan look. "Tell her."

Jamil nodded. "It's true. He is wildly unfunny."

"Then why have I not heard of this Obsidian Spindle?"

Teddy sniffed in the air. "Cuz even though you're a monster, like me and Jamil, you haven't been around many of us in your life, have you?"

I shook my head. "No."

"Well, there you go. Trust me when I say that the Obsidian Spindle is a real place, and it's inside the Dream Realm. The Dream Realm gets its power from the dreams of humanity, and the Obsidian Spindle is the most powerful object there. It's the only way to wake up your dear girlfriend."

"So, what? I fall asleep and just...search for it?"

"It's a might bit more complicated than that, I'm afraid," Teddy said. "You can get there, but it's quite dangerous."

"But that's where Rose is right now?"

"I reckon, and you have to work quickly to find her inside the Dream Realm before something happens to her. The Dream Realm is a dangerous place. If you die there, you die everywhere. And if you die here, you're stuck there forever."

"Die here? You mean if she doesn't wake up—"

"If her body lets loose her mortal coil before her soul reconnects with it, she'll stay in the Dream Realm. The body is strong, but it can't survive without a soul for long."

"Then how do I get there?"

Teddy stood up. "I could tell you, for a price."

I lowered my head. "I don't have any money."

"I don't want your money. I want your blood. Gorgon blood is especially tasty, and rare. It will power me for months. I do so hate feeding on french-fry gorging freshmen. Let me taste your blood, and I'll tell you where to go."

"That's crazy," I turned to Jamil. "That's crazy, right?"

Jamil pulled her shirt down to expose her right shoulder. There were two puncture marks there. Long healed, but they left a scar. "Afraid not. How much do you want to help Rose?"

I turned to Teddy. "How much does it hurt?"

"Not at all. Most people say it's even pleasurable."

I pulled my shirt down below my shoulder. "Do it quick. This better be worth it."

"It will, I guarantee it." Teddy took off his glasses and opened his mouth. With his fangs extending from his mouth, his grin was sinister. "Now, don't move. I wouldn't want to kill you."

With that, he sunk his teeth deep into my shoulder. I expected to wince, but instead a warm sensation radiated through my body. I started to giggle.

CHAPTER 10
ROSE

I landed on the ground with a loud thud. It didn't hurt, even though I had been falling for hours. Why didn't it hurt? When I trip and fall it hurts for days and leaves a big bruise, but now, after falling hundreds of miles, it felt like as soft as landing on a plush pillow.

I ran my hands along the grass under me as the breeze swept through my hair. I took a deep breath and smelled the lilacs and marigolds mixed with the sweet scent of freshly cut grass.

Wait.

Where was I?

I wasn't supposed to be here. I was supposed to be in school. I was supposed to be in the gym bathroom.

What happened? It was all hazy in my memory. I was looking into the mirror. Then I grabbed onto the—

This was a dream.

This was all a dream.

Oh, good.

I would wake up soon.

But when?

I had been in this place for hours. Never had I dreamed so vividly, or for so long.

"You can't be here," a hoarse voice cried behind me. "Move along."

A grumpy beaver wearing overalls over its unkempt fur pushed an old lawn mower. With just a few more rotations, his push mower's blades would run me over.

"Excuse me, Mr. Beaver, but where am I?" I said, scratching my head.

"You're on my lawn. Now, I've been polite, but if you don't move along, I'm going to run you over with my mower." The beaver moved steadily toward me, his push mower turning over with each step.

"I'm sorry, I'm not talking about—"

"I'm not stopping," the beaver said, taking another deliberate step forward.

"You're very rude. Did you know that?"

The beaver threw his paw in the air. "I'm not the one taking a nap on another person's property, am I?"

"I wasn't napping!" I yelled. "I landed here and you're being very impolite about it."

"A likely story." The beaver was quite close and clearly had no intention of stopping, so I jumped out of the way. I didn't notice the ditch beside me, though, and when I landed at the edge of it, my foot slipped from under me and I tumbled to the bottom.

"This is the weirdest dream I've ever had," I muttered as I stood up and brushed myself off. I wasn't wearing my sleep clothes. Instead, I wore a blue dress with a white apron, like the old Alice in Wonderland cartoons I used to watch as a child. It was the most curious thing, and it kept getting curiouser and curiouser.

"I have no idea what's going on here, but I'm certainly going to find out."

CHAPTER 11
CHELLE

"How long does it take to heal from a vampire bite?" I asked as we walked across campus. The blood was still seeping from my wound, but I was just glad it didn't gush. Teddy had plenty of gauze and bandages to fix me up after he finished harnessing my blood.

"Less time than you'd think," Jamil replied. "By tomorrow morning, it should be fine."

"That soon?"

"Magic, man. It's crazy. Something about Teddy's saliva that makes it heal faster. Like Neosporin."

"He'd make a fortune if he bottled it."

Jamil smiled, opening the door to her car. "Who's to say he didn't? How do you think he got so rich?"

I opened the passenger side door. "I don't know. I figured after a million billion years he would just have made a couple wise investments."

"He probably did that, too, but he made a killing selling his saliva to rich, white women as a cure all. They literally bathe in his spit at $1,000 a pop."

"That would be disgusting, if it wasn't so hilarious."

The address Teddy gave us was in Fresno, about two and a half hours from Sacramento. He told me that the man working the counter would help me get to the Dream Realm. When I pressed him about how, he clammed up and forced us to leave. I didn't even know the person's name we were looking for.

After a long drive, we pulled up to the address Teddy gave us. It was at the end of a derelict road, on the corner of a run-down strip mall. The brick façade was crumbling, and piles of ruddy bricks lined the ground in front of the shop. Based on the discolored stains left on the discolored window, I could tell the sign out front once clearly said "Pet Shop," but now the letters in the window only said "ET S OP."

"There is no way whoever's in there is going to help us get Rose back," I said, staring in disgust at the building.

"Maybe," Jamil said, opening the car door. "But if we don't try, then you let Teddy suck your blood for nothing. Not to mention, we drove to Fresno for nothing. *Fresno.* I for one never thought I would be caught dead in this town. If we don't at least go in and try, I might just drop dead from shame."

"Fine," I said, getting out of the car. "But I don't have to like it."

"Bitch. I have no dog in this fight and I'm here. I don't want to hear ANY of your mouth."

I couldn't disagree with her. Jamil was a decent friend, but she didn't know me particularly well. She was more friendly with Rose than me, but that was usually the case. People tended to love Rose, and Rose loved people. Meanwhile I hated everybody, and everybody kept their distance from me.

When I pushed open the pet shop door, I left a handprint on its thick layer of dirt. The grime came off on my hand, and I wiped it on my pants with a groan.

"Hello," a slender man said from the back of the store. He was ganglier than I thought possible for a human, but then I assumed he probably wasn't a human at all—not if he could help us. His arms hung low, all the way to his knees, and his face sagged as if the muscles had been eaten away.

"Hi," I said, walking up to the counter. The cages in the store were all empty and the haunting silence made each one of our steps echo off the walls. There wasn't one animal in the store, except for a small white rabbit on the counter that the slender man pet continuously.

"How may I help you?" the man said. He attempted a smile but lacked the musculature. "I'm afraid we're short on stock, but I can special order anything you would like. People just don't come to pet stores like they used to, I'm afraid. It's very sad."

"Sure," I said, not sure how else to respond. "But I am hoping you can help me. Do you know a Teddy?"

The man raised his slinky arm up to his chin. "It's possible. There was a time that my store was quite popular. In those days, I knew all sorts of people.

"He's a vampire," Jamil added.

The man nearly choked. "A vampire, you say? My friend, I think you are reading too many fairy tales."

Jamil shook her head. "No. I don't think so." She pointed to the amulet on her necklace. "You recognize this, right? I can see you wear one as well."

I did a double take to see that, sure enough, the pet store owner was wearing the same amulet as Jamil. His had an opal in the core instead of a ruby. Teddy had given me one with an emerald inside of it, but I had yet to put it on.

"This is just a trinket," the pet store owner replied dryly.

"What are you?" Jamil said.

The pet shop owner pressed his hands on the counter in front of him and leaned forward. His long fingers clasped the edge of the counter. "You show me first."

I didn't like to show myself in public, or to new people, but as Jamil made it abundantly clear, my disguises weren't very good. With a swipe of my hand, I pulled off my wig and shook my hair free.

The snakes which had been lulled into slumber by a sleeping charm woke up and hissed at the pet shop owner.

"My my," he said, intrigue oozing with every word. "A gorgon. I thought you were all extinct."

"Lots of people are trying to make it that way," I replied. "But I'm not dead yet."

"And what about you?" the pet store owner said to Jamil. "I can smell magic all over you."

Jamil removed her amulet to reveal her wooden, dryad form. "Happy now?"

"Never," the man said. "However, it is so nice to see you for what you really are. It warms my cold, dead heart."

"And what are you?" I asked him.

"Regrettably, I am a human. Or, at least stuck in human form. Once, I made a deal for a soul, and learned it was a trap only too late. Since then, I have been trapped in this miserable, vulnerable form, trying to keep it alive until I find a way out."

Jamil studied the shop owner up and down before her eyes lit up in surprise. "Are you a demon?"

The demon bristled. "That is a pejorative term for my kind. You can call me Etsop."

I looked back at the door, at the only letters left on it. Et s op. "Well, you aren't hiding very well."

"I've long since stopped caring about hiding. Those that seek me out are few and far between, and their proclivities often get themselves killed without me having to do anything about it."

"Well," Jamil said. "I'm afraid we're not much different."

"Of course you aren't. You mortals are all the same, no matter the manner of monster." He leaned over the counter and rubbed his hands together. "Anyway. What can I do for you?"

"We need to get my girlfriend to wake up from the Dream Realm. She's lost there."

Etsop raised his eyebrows. "It's a very dangerous place, you know."

"I don't care." I shrugged. "I have to rescue her, no matter the cost."

The demon placed his hands on either side of his mouth and curled his lips up into a cruel, disgusting smile. "In that case, I might be able to help you."

CHAPTER 12
CHELLE

The demon Etsop led us out to the front of his store. When he looked around to make sure nothing was watching him, he didn't turn his head. His whole body turned when he moved, as if he was scared to break his brittle bones. "You can never be too careful. Not with these frail human bodies."

"What are you doing?" Jamil asked.

"Just be patient. You younglings need to know everything so quickly. I run a business and wouldn't get very far if I mistreated my customers. It will all be revealed soon enough." He pulled a long pole from its holster on the side of the building and used it to reach toward the roof. "Come on."

I heard something latch above me. Etsop pushed the pole higher, and a large zipper appeared on the top of the store. "There we go."

As Etsop pulled the zipper, the front of the store dropped away. In the place of the crumbling façade was a blue and green neon tapestry with a woven door in the center. Night fell over us, and once the zipper was on the ground, all that I could see of Jamil and Etsop were the illuminated pupils of their eyes, their teeth, and their fingernails.

"Come this way," Etsop said, opening the door to the shop again. This time when I entered, dozens of different animal screams filled the air—animals of all types, though I had never heard their cries before on Earth.

"Where are we?" I asked.

"My store, of course."

"I've been to your store." I raised an eyebrow. "It suuuucks."

"Think of this as my other store. While the pet business is not very lucrative, my business helping the magical creatures of the world is booming."

I stopped to look at a glowing bird behind wrought iron bars. It looked like a parrot, but fatter, with razor sharp teeth poking out of its beak.

"It's way cooler than your other store."

"Don't touch anything," Etsop said, slapping my hand when I tried to pet the bird. "Not only are they prohibitively expensive, but many will also lead you to alternate dimensions, or send you straight to Hell, or fill you with an incurable disease which would kill you very painfully."

"We don't have a lot of money," Jamil said. "So, I'm hoping we can work out a deal."

"A deal," Etsop said, sliding behind the counter with a chuckle. "With a demon? Well, I've never heard of such a thing."

"Funny," I said.

"I'm kidding, of course." Etsop placed his hands on the counter in front of him. "I'm sure we can work something out. After all, you are only looking for information, and information is incredibly cheap in this day and age. The real money is in ingredients for incantations."

"So, we don't need an incantation to get to the Dream Realm?"

"No, all you need is to find the right door." Etsop pulled a crystal ball out from under the counter. "First, though, what we need to do is find where your friend is located. Do you have anything of great sentimental value that I could use to track her down?"

I looked down at my wrist. Rose had given me a friendship

bracelet when we first started dating. I thought it was corny at the time, but never once took it off. I reached down and yanked it off my hand. "Here you go."

Etsop held the string bracelet over the ball. He mumbled something I couldn't understand, and then his eyes rolled back in his head, leaving only the whites pulsing with white light in time with the ball.

"Oh, good," Etsop said, massaging the ball. "She is in Critterton. That is the nicest and least threatening place in the whole of the Dream Realm."

"That's good. That's good, right?"

"Very good, unless—oh, no. Oh dear."

"What is it?"

Etsop's eyes rolled back to the front of his head. "Well, it seems the Wicked Witch has learned of your friend's entrance into the Dream Realm, and even now works to find her."

"The Wicked Witch. You've gotta be kidding. That's a character from a fairy tale."

"That's just the name given to her by others. Her real name is Nimue, and she is the queen regent of all of the Dream Realm. She has been trapped there for centuries and longs to return to our world. She covets dreamers above all others, as she believes them the secret to her returning to Earth." Etsop leaned in toward me and spoke in a harsh whisper. "I'm afraid you must hurry, or your paramour will be lost forever."

"Then I need to enter the Dream Realm and get her to the Obsidian Spindle immediately." I stood up straight and looked around, searching for something to help me get there.

"You know of the Spindle. Good. Very good. That saves us a lot of time." Etsop held up a long, pointed finger. "I have a list of entrances into the Dream Realm. Be careful, though. While there are many doors into the Realm, there is only one door back out. Once you're in, you must go to the Obsidian Spindle, for that is where the exit is. Understood?"

I nodded. "I understand. Where am I going?"

Etsop faltered and gave a slight cough. "First, the manner of your payment. I will offer this information on one condition. Someday hence, I will call on you to perform a favor. This favor will not harm anybody you love or care about, nor will it get you arrested or killed. However, you must carry out this favor without question, and follow it to the letter. Agreed?"

"And if I don't?"

Etsop cleared his throat. "Then I will get angry. And you will not like me when I'm angry."

There was no other option. "In that case, I accept."

"Very good," he said, pulling out a big book from under his counter. "Now, let's begin."

CHAPTER 13
ROSE

The woodland creatures in the forest town tracked me warily as I walked down the sidewalk. The animals, ranging from squirrels and gophers to black bears and deer, scurried out of the way as I passed them. I heard them muttering to each other angrily.

"Excuse me?" I asked a kind-looking grizzly bear. She was wearing a bonnet and reading glasses as she hobbled in my direction, blissfully unaware of my presence. Lost in thought, she hadn't registered me yet. When she did, she nearly jumped out of her skin.

"Human!" she shouted in a high pitched, shrill voice.

"Shut up!" a badger in a three-piece suit hissed. "Do you want to alert the Queen's Guard?"

"What's the Queen's Guard?" I asked, inching toward the cowering bear.

"Why—what—how—" the badger stammered.

"It's okay, Bernard," the bear said, waving the badger off. "I will handle it."

The badger walked away, shaking its head. "Going to kill us all, she will."

The bear turned from the badger and gave me an incredulous look. "You truly are daft, yes?"

"I'm not daft. I'm just...new."

The bear sighed. "You should come with me, before they see you. Who knows what will happen if you stay out in the light of day?"

She grabbed my hand with her massive paw and pulled me off the path, squeezing between two houses. I couldn't have resisted following if I wanted to. The bear was excessively strong, and even if I struggled, it was clear that there would be no help from me from the other critters in town. I had no choice but to hope for the best.

The bear opened the front door of a little yellow house—much too small for her to enter comfortably—and threw me inside. A moment later she crouched down to enter and slammed the door behind her.

"A human. Here. Of all places," the bear said, scuttling over to the stove and turning on a burner. She placed a kettle under the faucet and when it was full, she slid it onto the fire. "Tea?"

"No, thank you," I said. "Maybe answers to a few questions, though."

She wheeled around to face me, jabbing the air with a teacup. "Of course you want something. That's all you humans want—something! All we want is to be left alone, but that's too much to ask, isn't it?"

I backed away slightly, taking a seat at one of the wooden chairs by the small, white table. "Who is we?"

"The Woodland Creature Society of Urgu. We have a binding agreement with the queen that no humans can enter the Dream Realm through our portal. I thought we were making progress. We hadn't seen one of you in over a hundred years. But now—well, just look at you!"

"Dream Realm? Portal?"

The kettle steamed and the bear filled her teacup, then a second one for me. She crossed the small room and sat down. The wooden chair creaked under her weight, but it didn't break. "Here."

"I didn't want any tea," I told her.

"And I didn't want to deal with you today, so it looks like we both get something we don't want. Drink."

I took a sip, and suddenly my whole body felt warm and tingly all over, as if I had just finished a long kiss with Chelle. "This is...wow, this is really good."

"I know. I'm very good with a kettle."

I placed the tea down and looked up at the bear. "I still don't understand. What is the Dream Realm?"

The bear lifted her eyes to the ceiling, shaking her head. "And here I thought we could just enjoy a spot of tea before getting into it, but I suppose we'll go at your schedule. You humans are all alike." She set down her tea. "You are in the Dream Realm right now, obviously. There are many portals all around the Dream Realm, but yours led you here, to Critterton."

"Yes," I said, after taking another sip of tea and waiting for it to make its tingly way down to my belly. "That makes some sense, I suppose...well, not really. I think I'm getting it, but...why am I here?"

"Why are any of us here?" The bear waved a philosophical paw.

I nodded. "That's a good question. Why are you here?"

"I am a unique case. I came because a child named Lucy dreamt me up several centuries ago and then died in her sleep. I will remain here until I am dusted."

"So, is everything here a dream?"

The bear shook her head. "Don't be silly. Most everything here is real. Urgu—sorry, that's what we call the Dream Realm—is filled with people and monsters who died in their dreams." She sighed. "I did not expect to give a history lesson today. I retired some time ago from the school, and you are quite a bit more annoying than my usual students."

"I'm sorry. You must understand I'm very, very confused."

"Quite, I would imagine. It's not every day you fall into the Dream Realm. Though, I'm not sure I'm going to make you feel any better about it, honestly. I am, in the end, only a bear."

"Please try...I'm sorry. I just realized I don't know your name."

The bear smiled. "It's Ursa."

I chuckled. "That's the name of a bear on Earth, too."

"I know. The child who dreamed me up wanted to befriend that bear, and so, she did, in her way."

"Well, Ursa, please. Tell me anything about this place."

"I wouldn't know where to begin."

"Well, why do dreamers come here at all?"

Ursa leaned forward and narrowed her eyes. "Were you ever told, in your youth, that everybody is born with a spark of the divine?"

"Sure, something like that. But that's just an old wives' tale, something they taught us in church."

"Not an old wives' tale. Many things have been lost in translation between the history of the universe and the religions that try to make sense of it, but that part is true. Everyone is born with a spark of the divine."

"I don't believe you, Ursa, and I am prone to believing most things."

"That's too bad, because it's the truth," she said, leaning back and sipping her tea. "The gods placed a spark of themselves inside of you when they molded humanity out of the universal clay. However, while your minds are strong, they made your bodies brittle and weak so you could not rebel against them. You cannot contain their spark for long. As it builds inside of you, your body fights to keep it controlled, but if it builds too great, then you will simply die."

"Curious."

"The Dream Realm was the god's solution to that problem. Every night, when you dream, your soul travels here into the belly of Urgu. The excess energy from that spark of the divine is deposited here, in the Dream Realm, and that spark powers everything in our world. Then, when you have deposited everything, you return and wake up."

I set my teacup down. "That sounds farfetched, even for a talking bear."

Ursa shrugged. "Maybe, but it's also the truth. Everything, even that tea you're drinking, is powered by the spark of a billion people built up over thousands of years."

"Okay, then why am I not going back to Earth? Why am I still here?"

The bear's eyes dropped to the ground and she was quiet for a moment. "You must be in a coma, or dead. When the soul has no body to return to after it deposits its spark, or cannot wake its body, it ends up here. There are makings of the imagination here in Urgu, like me, but most of its citizens are monsters, or humans like you, who either fell into a coma or died in their sleep."

"If bodies can just end up here, why am I so special?"

Ursa shook her head. "You're not special, dear. You're a nuisance. We filed a grievance with the queen to prevent humans from coming through our portal to the Dream Realm, and it was honored until this very day. Honestly, humans believe they are special. You're just another dead girl lost in Urgu. The problem is—"

I was quiet for a few moments, mulling all this over. Truth is, my thoughts were racing, and I could hardly breathe. "I...can't be dead."

"Did I say dead? I'm sorry. I might have misspoke. You might be dead, of course. You might not be. You'll never know. The only ones to know for sure are the Fates at The Obsidian Spindle, they are the only ones who can send you home. It's a long and treacherous road to meet them, but if you survive, they will grant you one wish."

I stood up. "How do I get there?"

Ursa looked up at me, surprised. "Through the woods, but you don't want to go there. The woods are—"

A crash from outside made the bear turn toward the window. The house next door was on fire. I looked up to see a scaly, two-headed dragon blowing fire down on the town.

"Dragons!" I shouted, backing away from the window. "There are dragons out there!"

"Oh no," the bear shrieked, her eyes darting between the door and the window. Her hands shook uncontrollably, until her teacup fell out of her hand and smashed onto the ground. "The Queen's Guard..." she uttered breathlessly. "They have come for you."

"What do I do?" I said.

"Pray," the bear said. "If they find you, you will become the property of the Wicked Witch, and subject to her experiments. She has been obsessed with dreamers since she came here, and now she hunts for you."

CHAPTER 14
CHELLE

Etsop opened the back door of his store. It led to a tunnel of sorts, where the ground was black, and the only light was a small dot in the distance.

"Where are we?" I asked, breathlessly. The darkness weighed on me so heavily it nearly brought me to my knees.

"The Nightmare Realm. It is a gateway between Hell and Earth, and the only place I feel at home."

"The Nightmare Realm?" Jamil asked.

Etsop nodded. "Just like dreams, nightmares exist outside of the universe. However, while the Dream Realm is fueled by happiness and light, this place is fueled by darkness, and that darkness is growing more powerful by the day."

"Why?"

Etsop shrugged weakly. "There used to be balance between the realms of light and dark, but now the door to the Dream Realm is closed to all dreamers, all dreamers except your Rose apparently. Everyone else, well, they have no choice but to end up here, in the Nightmare realm, fueling Epiales, the trickster god who rules here."

"Is that why everything is so messed up on Earth?" Jamil asked.

"Messed up?" Etsop asked. "I quite like it here."

"Well, I'm sure it's great for a demon, but like...have you looked around at everything that's happening on the news? It's like the whole world has gone mad."

"Feels the same to me as it's always been," Etsop replied. "But if this place has gone to pot, then it is a good bet that nothing will get better here until the balance is restored. Of course, I relish the darkness, so I hope it consumes everything."

"Enough," I said. "I'm not here for a history lesson. Why am I entering the Nightmare Realm?"

"It is the quickest way through to find the door into the Dream Realm. Doors connect the Nightmare Realm to Earth, as well. They won't open for most, but I have been given special dispensation from the dark lord."

"Why?"

"I was his lover once, before I was trapped in this hideous body. Epiales felt pity for me, so he allows me travel between his realm and Earth." Etsop placed his spindly hand on my shoulder. His fingers glowed for a second, and I felt a warm energy flow down my back. "I have given some of that power to you, for a time. Use it quickly, or you will be stuck here forever."

"I will try. Where am I going?"

"Do you see that?" Etsop said, pointing his spindly hand toward the light.

"Yes," I said. "It's about the only thing that I can see in this dark."

"Don't take your eyes off of it. That light will take you to where you need to go. When you get there, speak with Mydnyte, concubine of Nox. If she deems you worthy, she will open the door for you."

"And if not?"

"Then, she will eat you whole."

"Binary," Jamil said, behind me. "I like it."

I turned to her. "Are you sure you won't come with me?"

"After hearing that, yeah, I'm doubly sure." Jamil nodded empathically. "Besides, I have work to do, and classes to attend. Plus, I can check in on Rose if I go back."

"Can you take notes for me?" I said, hugging her. "Please?"

"I'll try. No promises. You probably won't come back, anyway."

"I'm coming back."

Jamil chuckled. "I like your confidence. I'll do what I can. Promise."

I turned back to the door and took a deep breath. "Then off I go."

"Remember," Etsop said. "Don't lose the light, or you will be lost in the Nightmare Realm forever."

I took a step out of the door and it slammed closed behind me. I wanted to look back, but knew in doing so, I risked losing the light. Something squished under my feet when I took a step, but I kept my eyes on the light.

With every step deeper into the darkness, my skin grew colder until even the swaying of my arms was agonizing, like my limbs were succumbing to frostbite. The wind whipped around me, and I saw in it twisted and demented faces, no doubt the faces of damned souls caught in the Nightmare Realm.

They whispered and chattered to me. "Give up." "Stop." "You will never be worthy." More and more of them floated into my ears and weakened my resolve, but I kept pressing onward toward that light in the distance.

"Watch out."

I had hardly even processed the voice when, just like that, I tripped over something. I snapped my head up and looked down the tunnel, but the light was gone. I pushed myself to my feet, scanning the darkness all around me. "No! No! Bring it back! Bring back the light!"

The cackles of the damned filled my ears and my soul grew heavy. They were right. I would never be worthy. I should just stop here. I should curl up in a ball and fade away.

"Enough!" I heard in a booming voice. I recognized it instantly as my mother's.

I whipped around. "Mom?"

Out of the darkness came a glimmer of light. First, her long snake-like tail came into focus, and then her scaly arms, and finally, her head, replete with a dozen snakes ten times longer than mine. Long fangs peeked out beneath her lips. She flicked one of the snakes away like stray bangs and murmured, "Seriously, they are so annoying. All they do is bicker all day."

"Mom!" I shouted, running toward her. My arms wrapped around what I thought was her waist but all I felt was cold air, and I stumbled through the ghostly form of her.

"Don't run too far from me. You have no idea how hard it is to find anything in the Nightmare Realm. Take my word for it. It's very difficult."

"What are you doing here?"

"Well, I'm dead, my love, and the dead have to wind up somewhere, don't they?"

"I suppose so, but I didn't realize the Nightmare Realm was the afterlife."

"This wasn't my first choice. I hear that in Hell, they let monsters torture the dead. That would be much more fun. Unfortunately though, when you die in your sleep, there are only so many options."

I had never known how my mother died, just that she was taken by monster hunters. They only ever found pieces of her body. The rest of her was skinned for parts. Gorgon tails alone are worth $100,000 on the black market.

"I didn't know. They only found part of your body."

"I'm not surprised. Butchers they were, the ones that took me. Not much I can do about it now."

I sniffled, trying to fight back my emotions. "They've come for me, too, several times."

My mother put her hand to her mouth. "Oh, child. I'm so sor—"

"It's fine," I replied, choking back a tear. "It's our lot in life, right?"

She sighed. "I never wanted that for you. I thought—I thought maybe with a human father you would—have a chance at a normal life."

I bit my lip. "Yeah, well, normal went out the door when you died —But it's fine. It's fine. I'm...fine."

Mom caught my eyes. "Don't lie to me, child."

I clenched my fists tightly. "Please, just let me, okay? There's nothing you can do about it, and there's nothing I can do about it. We just have to deal with our lot in life."

A slight smile grew across her face. "You truly are my daughter. You're right. No matter how bad our lot, we must deal with it with a stiff upper lip. After all, I thought I would be in the Dream Realm but—"

"The Dream Realm! That's where I'm going. Why aren't you there?"

"Because I died during a nightmarish hallucination. Those that took me needed me alive while they harvested my organs. The magic that courses through our veins becomes less powerful if harvested after death, so they placed me into a coma while they worked. Merciful, that bit, at least I didn't feel any pain."

"Don't give those butchers any credit. But...if you were asleep why didn't you enter the Dream Realm?"

"Urgu has not opened itself to dreamers in a century. Now every dream is a nightmare, and every dreamer ends up here. Nobody has seen the Dream Realm since Hypnos was vanquished and Hera took over, and her progeny, the Wicked Witch, Nimue."

"I don't get it. Wouldn't people know that there weren't dreams anymore? I swear I dream all the time."

"You haven't lived long enough to remember dreams. None who are alive now do. All you know is what you think are dreams, but I assure you, they are not."

Mom let out a deep sigh. "There used to be a balance between nightmares and dreams. However, with every passing day the Nightmare Realm collects more of the divine spark and grows more powerful. The balance is weakening, and soon, the Nightmare Realm will overpower everything, including the Dream Realm."

"That sounds like it's a big problem, and one that needs to be addressed, but it's a little over my head right now. Right now, I just need to save Rose. Etsop used a crystal ball to locate her and said that she's in the Dream Realm. I need to get there."

"Who's Rose?"

My mother had died before I started dating. She didn't even know I was gay. "She's my girlfriend."

"Oh?" Mom said. She didn't waver for a second about my sexuality. She just smiled. "Does she treat you well?"

I nodded. "Very well. I love her. That's why I can't lose her."

"That's good. I'm glad you are happy."

"Well, happiness is relative."

"Treasure what you have. Happiness is a fickle thing. You'll learn it never gets easier, even with time."

"That's depressing."

"My love, you are in the Nightmare Realm, trying to save your girlfriend. It doesn't get much more depressing than that." My mother turned away from me. "If she really is in the Dream Realm, you have little time to lose before the Wicked Witch finds her. She's obsessed with dreamers and thinks they are the key to changing her fate."

"And what fate is that?"

"She is fixated on escaping the Dream Realm. Nothing can leave that place, except for dreamers. Nimue has been experimenting on them for generations in order to find a way to leave for herself and her goddess, Hera."

"Hera, the god?"

"That's right. The mother of Gorgons. She is the reason we were given this accursed form. Once, we were beautiful—"

"We are still beautiful."

"Don't patronize me, dear. I know you don't believe that." Again, my mother smiled. "But I appreciate your small kindness."

"I do think you are beautiful, though. I just don't think I am."

"That is more of Hera's doing. I will never forgive her for what she did to me."

"How did she get locked in the Dream Realm?"

"She was imprisoned by Zeus for her mischievous ways. Only the Dream Realm and Nightmare Realm can hope to hold a god. The gods do not trust Epiales, and for good reason. He is tricky and a schemer. Even now I feel a plot brewing, but I have not been able to discern its nature. Hypnos was the much more trustworthy brother. He kept Hera contained for eons, until she overthrew him. Still, the Dream Realm has not bowed to her rule, nor have the Fates acquiesced to her demands to return to Earth."

"They are who I need to see. I need to find Rose and take her to the Obsidian Spindle so I can return her back to her body before it dies."

"A noble request. If I had one request of the Fates, it would be to kill Hera for cursing us with this hideous form."

"The Fates can kill a god?"

"They can cut any thread they choose."

"They really are the most powerful beings in the universe, then."

"Yes, but even power has its limits, and if you don't find your girlfriend soon, even the Fates won't be able to help her."

"Then I have to go quickly."

"Quite," my mother said. "*Iam accensas ad ostium revelare.*"

A bright light emanated from my mother's hands. She pushed it away from her body like passing a basketball, and it flew across the darkness. I saw the hideous faces of the damned souls as it skated across the plains. After a second, the light illuminated a door in the distance.

"Find that door and it will lead you where you need to go." My mother floated in front of me. "Be careful. The Wicked Witch is nobody to be trifled with."

"I'll try."

She gave me a warm smile. "It was so good to see you, my love. Now, go."

CHAPTER 15

CHELLE

The bright door from the Nightmare Realm spat me out on the corner of a dingy street in the middle of gods knew where. Angry people walked back and forth briskly, repeatedly banging into me.

"Excuse me!" I said.

"Yeah!" a black guy with a long, unkempt beard shouted back. "Excuse you!"

At least they speak English, I thought to myself. I glanced around, trying to catch my bearings. Before I could, a big, greasy hand pulled me from behind and yanked me into a nearby bodega.

"You come with a flash, aye?" a squat man with no neck and a red nose said. "Etsop just sending anybody through portals nowadays. Don't you know how to be discrete?"

I felt one of my snakes peak out from under my wig and pushed it back. "Apparently not. Some people say it's my biggest flaw."

The shop was small and cramped. There was no order to the food on the shelves. Bags of chips sat next to cookie dough, and cans of Dr. Pepper teetered on top of a rack of newspapers.

The man's bloodshot eyeballs looked me up and down. "You have bigger flaws."

"Thanks. I don't have enough anxiety as it is."

The man walked behind his counter and picked up a meat cleaver and used it to hack off the legs of a chicken. The pay counter also acted as a makeshift butcher shop, with different cuts of meat displayed in a glass case below him, and links of sausages hanging from above.

"You really think Mydnyte is gonna let you through that door?"

I shrugged. "Either that or she's gonna eat me."

The man chuckled. "I don't think you're her type. She doesn't like reptiles."

"I'm half-human."

"Maybe she'll only eat half of ya."

"Do you know where she is?"

The man looked up from his cleaving. "What's to say I'm not her? That's a very heteronormative definition of femininity."

"You are talking about her in the third person? Usually people don't do that about themselves"

"So? Maybe I ain't everybody."

"Are you her?"

"No."

"I didn't think so."

The man scoffed and shook his head. "I'm just saying...rude."

"I don't have time for this. Do you know where I can find her or not?"

He nodded. "I do. Or, that is to say, I know where the door is. Mydnyte's not far away from it, but I can never track her. Demonesses are wily, you know."

"Okay, so where is the door?"

"You get right to point, little one, don't you? Don't you know you catch more flies with honey?"

"Why would I want flies?"

"It's an expression."

"I know. I always thought it was stupid. I want flies to go away. So, tell me where she is, and I'll buzz off."

The man laughed ruefully. "She's gonna love you. Take the back door. Down the alley. You'll know it when you see it."

"Thanks."

"Don't thank me. You're in way over your head. If I was any kind of nice, I would tell you to let her go."

"Let who go?"

"Your love. You don't hide it very well. You need to hide it better with Mydnyte. If she smells love on you, she's going to gobble you up. There is only one thing she responds well to."

"And what's that?"

"Revenge."

"I'll keep that in mind."

The back door of the bodega led into an alley piled high with trash and dumpsters. The walls, an old brick façade, were riddled with graffiti. It stank of rotten meat so badly it was hard to keep from dry heaving.

I stepped over soggy boxes of cardboard and around overflowing dumpsters. Different doors lined the walls, leading into various buildings. I wasn't sure which door would take me to the Dream Realm, but the bodega owner seemed sure I would know it when I saw it.

And then I did. There, at the end of the alley, a door, torn from its hinges and resting against the side of a derelict building. Its frame was rotten to the core, and I doubted that it would even open for me. However, I was certain it was the right door.

I searched the sky and all around me for a demoness, but all I saw were rats scuttering around the alley. I sidled up to the door and placed my hand on the rusted knob. Turning it slowly and brushing off the rust that flecked off on my fingers, I opened the door, only to find nothing but hollow emptiness on the other side. There was nothing.

A childish voice cut through the air. "I have to bless it first."

I turned around but nobody was behind me. A black cat rushed across the alley and grabbed a rat trying to scurry through a hole in the wall to safety. There would be no safety for it, though, and it was caught in the cat's claws before it could disappear. As it brought the rodent to its mouth, the cat grew, doubling in size, and then doubled once more. Its paws became fingers, which became hands, and when it placed the rat in its mouth, the mouth turned from a cat's mouth to that of a human.

An alabaster woman with black eyes, dressed in a black gown, stared back at me from where the cat had been. The eyes had no white. They were completely onyx. Her teeth were sharp, and a forked tongue flicked the last specks of blood from her mouth.

"Mydnyte?" I asked.

"That's me," she said. "Are you another foolish mortal, come to unbind yourself from the coil that keeps you alive, and feed your spark to me?"

"No," I said, straightening my shoulders. "I am here to gain passage to the Dream Realm."

"To me, they are one and the same. I haven't granted passage in many moons." Mydnyte lunged toward me, but I didn't flinch. "I smell magic on you, mortal."

I pushed back my hoodie to reveal the snakes on my head. "I have been getting that a lot recently. I am a gorgon."

"Yuck," Mydnyte said, her lip curling. "I don't do reptiles."

"Good," I said, curtly. "Cuz I'm not here to be eaten."

"Why are you here?"

I thought for a moment. I thought back about what my mother told me about Hera, and how she is bound to the Dream Realm. "I'm here to kill Hera."

Mydnyte laughed and her screech filled the air. "That is rich. Very rich. What makes you think you can kill a god?"

"I can't," I replied. "But the Obsidian Spindle can, and when I get there, I will use the wish the Fates give to cut the thread that binds Hera's life."

"And why would you do that?" Mydnyte said, intrigued.

"It's easy. Gorgons used to be the most beautiful creatures on the planet. Look at us now. Loathsome creatures, hunted nearly to extinction, and I'm sick of being hunted."

"You have a certain charm to you. An acquired taste, to be sure, but I could find you beautiful."

"She cursed my mother. Monster hunters have chased us for generations. Hera needs to die, and I'm going to kill her."

Again Mydnyte laughed, taking a step closer to me when she finished. "You make me laugh, mortal. I know you are lying, but even the mere thought of killing Hera, and allowing me to leave this place, is more joy than I have had in eons."

"You're trapped here?"

"I am cursed to guard this door until Hera no longer needs to be bound within the Dream Realm."

"So, if she dies, you go free."

"That is the oath I made to the goddess Nox many centuries ago, when she granted me eternal life...for a cost. I did not know how high the price."

Mydnyte shut the door closed and tapped on it three times with the tips of her fingers. When she opened it again, I no longer saw the ground, but a beautiful forest overlooking a quaint town. However, all was not peaceful. Dragons flew over the buildings, burning them to ashes. Screams of agony filled the air.

"You better hurry," she said. "It looks as though great danger is afoot."

I didn't say another word. I ran through the door and into the Dream Realm. I would not let anything happen to Rose.

CHAPTER 16
ROSE

My new grizzly bear friend, Ursa, pushed me out of the house just as the roof lit up in flames from the breath of a navy-blue dragon. "Go!"

"Where?" I shouted.

"Away! Anywhere that's not here!"

The bear galloped on all fours. All around us were guards fighting with the peaceful critters. The soldiers wore full chain mail with swords and shields. It was like I had gone back in time four hundred years.

A cadre of fully-armored guards wearing green breast plates turned to Ursa and rushed her with their swords, but she barreled over them with little effort. Her "inner bear" unleashed, she turned to the guards and bellowed at them. I heard another shriek cutting through the air behind me just as a monstrous black dragon flew over and shot fire at her.

"No!" I shouted, but it was too late. The fireball exploded in front of Ursa and sent her flying into the air. The guards stepped away, leaving nothing but a charred bear laying in the middle of the street, still on fire.

I ran over to her and snuffed out her flames, then rolled her over carefully. She was barely conscious.

"I'm sorry. I'm so sorry."

"Go," was the last thing she said, before she vanished into thin air.

The dragon had turned around and was staring at me with its yellow, snakelike eyes. The sides of its mouth curled, and it swooped toward me. I spun around, but a dozen guards surrounded me, blocking my escape.

"Halt!" one of them said.

Suddenly, an echo rumbled across the ground, and the guard was flung a hundred yards through the air until he crashed into a house. Four more guards were tossed asunder and, in their wake, I saw her.

"Chelle!" I shouted, rushing toward her.

She grabbed my hand and pulled me away from the dragon, which sprayed fire inches from where I had been standing.

"Come on!" she said, as we sprinted between the fiery houses.

"Where are we going?" I asked, ducking a burning thatched roof.

"I don't know! Away from the fire!"

I saw the woods above the ridge that towered over the town. Ursa had told me it would take me where I needed to go. "There! Those woods lead toward the Obsidian Spindle!"

Chelle dragged me forward. "And they'll give us cover from this massacre. Let's go."

We scampered up the hill. I glanced behind us to make sure no one was following us. The guards were busy arresting pigs and skunks and other types of critters, and the dragons were having too much fun burning houses to look up at the tree line and notice our escape.

I felt bad for the harm I had brought upon the woodland creatures, but I couldn't help them. I could barely help myself. With one last tug on my arm from Chelle, I disappeared into the woods after her.

CHAPTER 17
RED

By the time I entered Critterton the whole town was on fire. Usually I would have fought for them, but I was there on a mission for Ozma. I didn't have time. Even if I did have the time, I wasn't sure there was anything I could do to help.

Find the dreamer and bring her to safety before the Wicked Witch finds and binds her. That was my mission. There hadn't been a new dreamer in the Dream Realm in over a hundred years. Not since Hypnos vanished, taking the secrets of the Realm with him.

The dreams that once powered this place had all but faded. I had heard talk that the Nightmare Realm was at its greatest power in untold millennia; there were hardships on Earth and the whole of civilization was collapsing before us. If we couldn't find a way to bring dreamers back to Urgu, it could be the end of all our worlds.

And this girl, whoever she was, could be the key to saving us all. I couldn't let the Wicked Witch capture her first. Not this time.

A pack of the Wicked Witch's guards passed by me. They were human, but barely. Long ago they had been promised their freedom from Urgu if they helped the Wicked Witch. Every day their souls became more and more corrupt, and they were entirely susceptible to the false queen's will.

That's why I had no trouble slaughtering them. I gripped my dual daggers tightly and sliced one across the neck and stabbed another in the stomach. They disappeared in my arms, nothing but ash and dust. Before they could raise their swords, I stabbed the other two soldiers straight through their chests and watched them turn to dust under my blade. What remained of them, the ash that made up their souls, blew away in the wind.

Two rabbits hopped past me as I ducked behind a flaming house. One of the Witch's guards grabbed at them, but I pulled a dagger from my thigh and stuck her with it. She collapsed to dust and the rabbits escaped down the garden path. They wouldn't be safe for long, but I had to do something to protect them.

In the town square, the usurper's army had collected the critters and bound them. A blue dragon sat perched on a stone fountain, gazing at them with a hungry look. The fountain was a gift from Ozma, from the days when critters were friends with humans, centuries ago.

A scar-faced guard screamed at a porcupine. "Tell us where she is!"

"We don't know!" The porcupine cowered.

The guard glared at the critters. "Araxis! Burn them!"

I turned away from the carnage. There was nothing I could do without giving away my position. Dragons were the one beast I dared not face, at least not alone. Screams echoed across the city until the poor little critters vaporized into dust.

"Find her!" the callous, scar-faced guard screamed.

The guards disbanded and spread out into the streets again. Two of them made their way toward me. I spun around the back of the house and stuck them both through the neck when they passed me. They disintegrated at my feet.

Now was my chance. The guards were busy searching the streets and the square was unguarded. The only thing keeping me from crossing the square was the dragon, and it was facing the other way.

I took a step toward the town's center and that's when I saw two figures running up the hillside toward the woods. One was a human. The other a gorgon. One of them had to be the dreamer. They were damned fools if they thought they could survive alone in the Enchanted Forest.

"Hey!" I heard from the side of the square. "It's th—"

I crossed the square in an instant and slit the guard's throat, who disintegrated in my hands. Two more guards were rushing toward me.

"It's you!" one of them snarled.

The other one aimed his spear. "The Red Rider!"

"That's right," I said with a smirk.

They stabbed at me with their spears, and I leapt over them. I threw a dagger into the first guard's eye and as the other charged, I swerved to dodge his spear then stuck him with another dagger right where his cold, dead heart would be, if he were still alive.

When they both had disintegrated, Araxis turned toward me and let out a bellow of fire. I fell to the ground to avoid it and rolled away from him. I couldn't take on a full-grown dragon. Maybe a youngling, but not one who had been in the service of the dark queen since before I came to Urgu.

The forest was my only way out without fighting my way through a battalion of the Wicked Witch's troops. I flung two throwing daggers from my shin toward the dragon, hoping to distract it for a moment, and then gunned up the hill and disappeared into the forest. I wondered how many guards had seen me enter. If they came for me, I would fight them in the brush. They would never burn the forest, though, and risk their already-uneasy alliance with the pixies, so I was safe from the dragon fire for the time being.

If I didn't find the dreamer soon, though, I feared she would be lost forever.

CHELLE

Rose held me for a full five minutes once we stopped, deep in the dark woods. When she finally pulled away, she kissed me gently.

"You came for me," she whispered.

"Of course I came for you. I will always come for you."

She smiled. "You've always said that, but I would be lying if I said I believed you."

"That's okay. I believed it enough for both of us."

A twig snapped in the distance, and the feeling of danger swirled in my stomach. I had been lost in my blissful reunion with Rose, and for a moment it was like we were on our own little island. That feeling had to go away if we wanted to survive.

"Come on," I said, grabbing her arm. "We have to get out of these woods."

"How?" Rose walked briskly through the brush. "We don't even know how to get to the Obsidian Spindle."

"I know the way," a squeaky voice chirped.

I looked around but didn't see anything. "Who are you? Show yourself."

"Our kind has made that mistake before, to our detriment. How do I know you are trustworthy?"

"We're very trustworthy," Rose said, nodding and looking around.

"So, I'm just supposed to take your word? That's gotten plenty of my kind killed."

I shook my head and started walking again. "Forget this. We'll figure it out ourselves. We don't have time for your games."

Dozens of pastel lights twinkled around us, like glowing raindrops suspended in the sky. "Don't you? There are many dangers in these woods. You have never been here before. I would recognize you."

"No, we haven't," Rose said, pausing to watch the lights.

"Don't encourage them," I said.

"Why not? If it's dangerous here, we need a guide."

I turned around to face her. "And what if she's lying to us?"

"I guess you'll just have to trust me," the voice said.

Rose ignored the voice, narrowing her eyes. "How is me trusting you different from you trusting me?"

"Easy. I know my way, and you don't. I could survive very easily without you, but I doubt the same can be said about you."

"That's not fair," Rose said. "We've survived this long."

The voice chimed in again. "And yet, you are even now being chased by the Queen's Guard and these are strange, unknown woods. Odds are, you won't survive much longer."

"She's right," Rose said.

Despite my disgust with the voice, I couldn't disagree. "Fine!" I said, stomping my foot. "How do we prove our trustworthiness?"

"Simply answer my questions honestly. If you do, I will reveal myself."

I gritted my teeth. "Ask your questions then."

"What brings you to the Enchanted woods?"

I eyed Rose, who cleared her throat before she spoke. "I fell into a coma and landed in that little critter village outside the forest."

"And I," I added, "came in to rescue her."

"Came through which door?"

"The one guarded by Mydnyte."

"She is very tricksy. What did you promise her?"

I didn't want to say that I promised to use my wish to kill Hera. I thought about biting my tongue and refusing to answer, or lying, but I had the feeling I'd be better off telling the truth.

"Before I tell you, I have a few questions for you."

"That is not how the game is played."

I gritted my teeth. "I. Don't. Care."

"Fine," the voice said. I swore I could hear its eyes rolling at me.

"What are your feelings about Hera?"

"She is a powerful goddess. Perhaps the most powerful one left now that Hypnos is no longer with us."

"And what about her regent, Nimue?"

"Our queen must be respected and obeyed, lest we lose our heads."

"Those aren't good answers," Rose said. "They are facts, not feelings."

"I like you," the voice replied. "Very well. I have no opinion on Hera. She is a god, like the others, and they are much the same; petty and cruel. Even Hypnos was not without his heartless indulgences, and when it suited his whims, he abandoned us without so much as a whisper, proving that we meant nothing to him. However, I am not a fan of our overlord. She came about her crown by ill-gotten gains, and we of the forest do not like that. We have lived by a strict code for thousands of years, and when one breaks their vows, we take notice."

"What vow did she break?"

"The witch used to be the royal advisor to our rightful queen, Ozma. Then, she fell into league with Hera, and changed. She forced Ozma from her throne and took it for herself. She is a liar and a cheater, and consorts with the most vile in our land, one for whom this land is a prison. Hera."

I took a deep breath. "Okay, I will tell you what I promised Mydnyte. I promised her that if I made it to the Spindle, I would use my request of the Fates to cut Hera's thread and kill her."

"Interesting...interesting," the voice said. "That is a very good wish."

Rose grabbed my shoulder and dug her nails in deep. "Are you kidding me? We need those requests if we're going to get home."

I smiled. "You can request we both go home, my love."

"Oh. I suppose I can."

The pastel lights turned into a bright white that illuminated the whole forest. I covered my eyes until the light faded, and when I looked again, hundreds of little pixies floated in the air around me, none more than six inches tall. Their faces were covered in sparkles and painted in every color under the sun.

"Very interesting," the voice said. It belonged to the pixie at the front of the pack. It was dressed head to toe in yellow, even on its wings, and accented with glitter.

"Very well, strangers. You have proven yourself useful to us Seelie folk."

"What's a Seelie?"

The sides of the pixie's mouth curled. "We are the good guardians of the forest. Come, follow me and I will lead you to our queen. You have much to discuss with her."

"Do we have a choice?" I asked.

"You could die in the forest," the pixie said. "Oh, bother. That sounded like a threat. I mean you no harm. I am Muirgen, ambassador to Queen Aine, wardeness of the Enchanted Forest and ruler of the magic folk."

Rose reached for my hand. "Come on, Chelle. What are you so nervous for?"

"I don't know." I gave the pixies a wary glance as I followed behind Rose. "It's probably nothing."

CHAPTER 19
RED

The Enchanted Forest was dark and filled with secrets. You could walk behind a bush and end up a hundred miles away if you weren't careful. I doubted neither the dreamer nor her companion were careful, given the circumstances. Even those who lived here for centuries had troubles navigating the verve. There were countless tales of people and monster alike vanishing into the woods, never to be seen again.

Usually, it had to do with Unseelie trickery. The Unseelie overthrew the Seelie queen, locking their pixie cousins in their dungeons and feasting on them one by one. Now, there were no Seelie left, so it made spotting the fakes easy. It was all trickery.

"Halt, rider!" a high-pitched voice squealed through the brush.

"I have no quarrel with you, pixie. I come for the girl and her gorgon compatriot. Give them to me and we will have no trouble here."

"Please," the voice said, and in a flash, a pink fairy appeared, holding a bow staff. "I know all about you and your mission for the false queen."

My fists tightened. "Ozma is the rightful ruler of Urgu, pixie, and I will not have you besmirch her name."

The pixie put her hands on her hips. "She lost her claim to the crown with the vanishing of Hypnos. Hera is the most powerful god that remains here and the only one who has claim to this land."

"The most powerful perhaps, but not the only. One day, we will unite the outer gods and take back the gold throne from her."

Golden glitter fell from her petulant face and landed on the ground. "Even with the other gods, you stand no chance against the throne. The Wicked Witch is too powerful, and Hera is behind her. We will unlock the Obsidian Spindle before long, and then return to the Universe more powerful than ever."

I moved toward the pixie, my eyes narrowing. "Is that what you were promised? That you could return to Earth if you sold your soul to the dark queen?"

"It is what we were all promised. Urgu is stale and boring. Humans no longer come here and tricking them is our only joy. On Earth, there are millions, even billions to torture."

"And what of the two that came through here? Did you trick them, too?"

"It wasn't much of a trick. They were desperate for help, and we were more than happy to lend false aid."

"Where are they?"

"At the castle now, I suppose. They'll be prisoners by nightfall. The Wicked Witch has already been called to deal with the dreamer. She and her men will be here before long."

"Then I have little time."

I pushed back my red cape and dug my hand into the pouch by my daggers. Inside was a mix of ground boxwood and iron shavings. On their own, both repel pixies, but together, they form a powerful barrier.

I balled up my fist and swung my arm forward, dispersing the boxwood and iron. As I did, the pixie nearest to me began to cough and the other pixie guards scattered to the winds. I reached behind my back and pulled out a glass bottle imbued with flecks of iron, perfect for catching a pixie. I swung my arm through the air, and one of the pixies fell inside, trapped.

"Let me out!" the pixie shouted at me from inside the bottle.

I peered into the bottle. "Take me to them, and you will be set free. Otherwise, you will spend your life in this jar."

"Fine," it said with a huff. "I hate you, though."

"I don't care."

CHAPTER 20
ROSE

The pixie Muirgen flew in front of us through the woods which looked, honestly, quite lovely. With her guiding us I knew that we would be okay. I was able to enjoy the pleasant stroll through the forest, which was filled with majestic trees and speckled with pixies floating as if they didn't have a care in the world.

Chelle shared neither my optimism nor sense of wonder. Instead, she walked with her eyes narrowed and jaw clenched, like she was waiting for a battle.

"Will you relax?" I said, squeezing her hand.

"I'm not going to relax until we get to the Obsidian Spindle and I get you home. We don't have time—"

"You keep saying that," I said. "Why do you keep saying that?"

"I don't want to tell you."

"Tough."

"Fine, but it's going to bum you out."

"I just got attacked by dragons, and I'm being led through the woods by pixies. I don't think you could bum me out any more or shock me with anything."

"You asked for it. Just remember that."

"I will."

"We're fighting a battle against time, Rose. If we don't get out of here before you die, back in the real world, you're going to be stuck in here forever."

I stopped. "Wait. Forever?"

"We really must be going," Muirgen said, floating back to us.

"In a minute," I said, turning back to Chelle. "What do you mean *die*?"

"I mean you're in a coma out there, but eventually, you're gonna die. The body can't last for long without the soul."

"Yeah, but I've seen people come out of comas after years, right?"

"Maybe, but maybe not. I have no idea how bad it's going to get for you. I have no idea what kind of condition you'll be in if we wake you up. But the longer we wait, the worse your odds for living a normal life if you do wake up."

"Oh," I said. "That does bum me out."

Honestly, I didn't mind being in Urgu, except for the death of my body part. My life wasn't exactly fun and exciting out in the real world. I was constantly struggling to make enough money not only to live, but to survive. I had maxed out my credit cards and my medical bills were going to bankrupt me for sure, and it's not like my parents were helpful.

But I couldn't just stay here forever. I needed to go back eventually, didn't I? Even if my old life was miserable.

"How far away are we?" Chelle asked.

"Not far. Just around this clearing and we'll be at the castle." Muirgen floated forward, expecting us to follow.

Chelle put her hand on my back. "Come on. We can fix this. I promise we're going to fix this."

I nodded. "I know. I'm just not sure I want it fixed."

"Yes, you do," Chelle grabbed my hand. "I'm not going back to Earth alone. I can't handle it there without you."

I smiled at her. "As long as we're together."

"We will be."

"Come on," Muirgen said, her voice strained. "You don't want to keep the queen waiting."

I didn't want to appear rude, so I listened to the pixie and quickened my gate, hopping up the makeshift rock staircase that led up the next ridge, though for the life of me I didn't know why flying pixies would need stairs.

"Here we are," Muirgen said when I reached the top of the hill.

Below us was a bright pink castle with four towers and a rainbow river flowing alongside it. Flags rose high into the air from the top of each tower. It was impressive and ornate, but there was a problem. It was no bigger than a Barbie Dream House, though at least ten times as garish and a hundred times as pink.

"Looks like my old Polly Pockets," Chelle muttered.

I giggled. "You had Polly Pocket?" The thought of Chelle having anything pink was comical.

"I wanted Mighty Max, but my mom got the wrong memo I guess."

I turned to Muirgen. "Chelle makes a good point. How are we, um, going to see the queen if we can't fit into the castle?"

"That's easy. I'm going to shrink you."

"Whoa, whoa." Chelle put her hand up. "There is no way I'm letting you use magic on me. Besides, how is something so small as you going to help us get to the Obsidian Spindle?"

Muirgen gasped. "That's so offensive. Our magic is more powerful than any in Urgu besides those who are God-touched. We may be small, but that just makes our magic concentrated."

"Come on, Chelle," I said. "You are a wet blanket. I've always wanted to shrink like Alice in Wonderland."

"I'm not being a wet blanket. You've never been around magical creatures except for with me, Rose. We're not all good guys."

"And you're not all bad guys, either." I smiled at Muirgen. "Shrink me!"

I had been around Chelle for a long time, but she had never used magic near me until now, in Urgu. Honestly, I had always been curious about it, even if I never said anything to her. I had hoped she would come to trust me with her magic.

"I'm not going," Chelle said. "They aren't using that stuff on me."

"Fine," I said. "I'm perfectly capable of parlaying with the queen on my own."

Chelle stared at me for a long time, biting her lips in deep thought. "Okay. If something goes wrong, I'll be here to get you out. But just know, I think this is a stupid idea."

"You think everything it a stupid idea."

"Are you ready?" Muirgen asked me.

"Absolutely. I can't wait to meet your queen."

"Very well then," Muirgen said, then she snapped her fingers. "I'll meet you in a moment."

My body shook and rumbled, and a great earthquake sound rattled through my ears. It felt like I was moving at a hundred miles an hour, but I was standing still.

The trees above me fell further away, except they didn't move at all. It was me that was shrinking, and shrinking, and shrinking. Chelle was a giant looming above me, and the castle turned from a tiny dollhouse to a towering monolith.

When I finally stopped moving, Chelle seemed a hundred feet tall. Normally, she was only a few inches taller than me, but now she could crush me under her boot in an instant.

"Hi Chelle!" I shouted, but she didn't hear me. I was too small.

I turned toward the castle. Its iron gates rose high into the air, and now that I was small, I noticed the intricate gilded spirals at the top of each bar. Two blue pixies stood guard with long spears. Their bodies glimmered even brighter now that they were my height. I looked down and watched the rainbow river shimmering in the sunlight as it flowed through the moat. I wondered how we would get across.

"It's not really a rainbow," Muirgen said. "It's the sun that makes it look that way."

I turned to see her, now my height, and noticed now that she was dressed in a three-piece suit, with a lapel pin in the shape of a butter-fly. Muirgen placed her hands behind her back and walked toward me.

"I hope you are more accommodating than your friend. The queen does not like to be disturbed, least of all by disrespectful monsters."

"Chelle's a lot nicer when you get to know her."

"Well, I have no intention of doing that," Muirgen said, walking to the edge of the moat. "Guards, lower the bridge!"

The guards turned to the levers on either side of the gate. They nodded to each other and pulled the levers at the same time. When they did, the great wooden bridge that protected the castle fell and allowed us to cross.

Muirgen hovered next to me as I walked over the bridge. "Why do you need a bridge if you can just fly?"

"You ask a lot of questions. Did you know that?"

"Yes," I nodded. "People think it's annoying."

Muirgen tittered. "Quite. Now, come along. The queen knows of your arrival, and we mustn't keep her waiting."

CHAPTER 21
CHELLE

"Don't look at me like that," I said to the dozen or so pixies buzzing around my head. "Don't you have anything better to do?"

They didn't answer. They just stared at me; their weapons drawn. Some had little swords, and others short lances, but they all were comically small compared to me. Still, I knew that pixie magic was strong. Even if their weapons were tiny, that didn't mean they couldn't hurt me— even kill me, if they got off a lucky shot.

"I'm sitting down now," I said, never taking my eyes off the pixies as I sat on a log next to the castle.

Pixies existed on Earth, too, but I had never run into them in the flesh. I had never seen talking critters or anything like that on Earth, either, but I suppose they could have existed. Pixies, however, I knew all about them, and how tricksy they were, down to the core of their being. Even the good ones were not to be trifled with, and the bad ones...well, you didn't want to tangle with them if you could help it.

"How long have you been here?" I asked out loud to no one in particular. I didn't receive a response. It was impossible to parlay with them if they didn't want to speak with me.

I hoped that Rose was okay. If these truly were the Seelie, they would ask her for a favor in exchange for helping her reach the Obsidian Spindle. When she completed the favor, they would concede to her request. But if these were Unseelie, then after she completed the favor, they would simply kill her.

Why did I let Rose go in alone? She had no magic, no power. She doesn't know anything about the world.

Actually, that's exactly why I let her go in alone. The favor they asked of her would be smaller for than what they would ask of me, as a magical creature. She would need to leave the castle to carry out the request of the queen, and then she would have to tell me what the favor was.

Of course, they might take her hostage, too. If she didn't come out, I would destroy the place, but I could only do so from out here. Strong, magical energy wafted from the castle. It was protected by powerful spells. If they shrunk me, I couldn't hope to generate enough power to break the shields. At my full size there was a chance I could match their might.

I didn't know much magic, but I was fluent in destruction and offensive magic. Smashing was my thing. At the very least, I could smash through, grab Rose, and run away. I would worry about getting her back into her true form later.

A twig snapped in the distance. Everyone, including the pixies, turned their attention to it. Pixies didn't walk, they flew, so it couldn't be one of them. Even if they were on the ground for some reason, they weren't heavy enough to break twigs.

A cloud of smoke billowed out from the clearing in front of us. The pixie guards coughed and started to fall to the ground, where they convulsed and spasmed.

When the dust settled and the pixies were silent, a woman dropped down from the hilltop. She wore a long red cape and held a bottle with a pixie inside. Her hair was dark red and matched her lips, but her skin was alabaster and her clothes black. She struck an intimidating figure against the forest.

"Are you the one that came here?" the woman said. "Are you the dreamer?"

She must have been from the Wicked Witch's army. I opened my hands and closed my eyes.

"*Flammis venit ad me.*"

My hands lit up with orange flame. Far from being frightened by the flame, the woman cocked her head. "Are you stupid? This is a forest."

"You won't take us without a fight."

"Yes. You are stupid. Thank you for answering me. I'm not here to take you. I'm here to rescue you."

"We're doing a fine job of that by ourselves."

"Are you? And where is your friend?"

"She's talking with the queen."

"The queen of the Unseelie! Are you crazy?"

"What do you mean, Unseelie? They said—"

"I know what they said," the woman said. "Damn it. The Unseelie are tricksters. You should know better, mage."

"And why should I trust you?"

"You're trusting everybody else. Why am I any different?"

"Good point," I said. "What do we do?"

"You do nothing. You'll just get her killed. I'll save her and bring her out of the castle."

"I'm here to save her, and I'm not just giving up on her."

The woman sniffed the air. "You smell...different. Why?"

"I'm a gorgon."

"I can see that, but that's not it. You reek of sweat like—" she paused, her jaw dropping. "You came into the Dream Realm with your body."

I blinked. "What?"

"You came here with your body. Do you have any idea how stupid that was?"

"Um...no?"

She pressed her fingers to her nose. "In order to enter the Dream Realm, one must deposit their god spark inside the core of this world. Nobody inside the Dream Realm has that spark left inside them. Nobody...except you. Since you didn't deposit your spark, it still flows inside you, making you the most powerful and dangerous person in all of Urgu. The queen is no doubt after you already, endangering us all."

"That's not my—"

"This might work to our advantage, though." The woman put down the glass bottle and tightened her cape. "You have your body, which means you have powerful magic. The pixies and the Queen's Guard will be looking for us. Keep them distracted until I get back."

"And what are you going to do?"

"Save your friend." She pulled a potion out of her pocket. "Don't burn down the woods while I'm gone."

The woman tilted back her head and drank down the potion in one gulp. A second later, she was the size of a thimble, and I watched her rush toward the castle gates.

"I guess I have no choice in the matter," I said, balling up my fists. I looked down at the pixie trying to escape the glass jar. "Just chill out, okay?"

CHAPTER 22

ROSE

I couldn't believe I was inside the castle I had seen from the outside, knowing it was the size of Barbie's playhouse. There was intricately detailed pink tile which rose into a point at the top of the room. Across the floor laid a long shag carpet of deep blue, almost black, and inlaid with a large, golden crest like those from the kings I learned about in European history class. These ones featured a pair of fairy wings in the middle of them, obviously denoting the royal house of the fairy queen.

"Can I ask you a question?" I asked Muirgen as we crossed the room.

"I suppose so," she replied. "Though you should keep your questions to yourself until you entreat with the queen."

"I don't think she would be able to answer this, or maybe it wouldn't be appropriate to ask her."

"Go ahead then," Muirgen said.

"How are you not scared all the time that everything is bigger than you?"

Muirgen let out a titter. "Well, we don't know any other way. Besides, while we are small, we are also mighty."

"Oh, of course. I would never think otherwise. However, the world is so scary for me, and I am much bigger than you. When I saw Chelle's foot, for instance, I knew she wouldn't hurt me, but I couldn't help but be frightened that I would get stepped on."

"Nobody would dare step on a pixie. If they did, they would face dire consequences."

We were silent, approaching the large, golden throne decorated with golden dragons. It loomed over us, raised high by a set of stairs.

On the throne sat a purple pixie wearing a golden headdress half as long as her whole body. Under her eyes were layers of golden paint, and her robe was woven of the same gold.

"Great Aine," Muirgen said, kneeling, "I bring you one who wishes an audience with you. She is—" Muirgen looked at me. "Kneel."

"Right," I said, dipping my knee to the ground and bowing my head. "My apologies, your majesty."

Muirgen nodded slightly at me, before retreating backwards to allow the queen to address me directly.

"Who are you?" Queen Aine asked, disdain dripping from her every syllable. "And by what right do you enter my kingdom?"

"I am Rose Blair, my queen. I did not mean to enter your forest. I am only looking for a way to the Obsidian Spindle and was told this was the quickest route."

The queen let out a great *harrumph.* "Yes, you and everyone else on the gods-forsaken continent. What makes you think you are worthy to speak to the Fates?"

My stomach sank to the floor. "I do not think I am worthy. I didn't know...worthiness had anything to do with it."

"Of course it does. The Fates do not grant the requests of anyone they encounter. If that were the case, then every inhabitant of Urgu could return to Earth."

"Is that what you want, your majesty? To return to Earth?"

"It is what we all want!" she thundered. "Urgu is but a waystation between life and death. It is never-ending nothingness, the same doldrum day after day."

"But...you are a queen," I said meekly once she was finished. I was trying to remain respectful, while also pointing out maybe she was being negative. "You must have more than just doldrum to entertain you."

"Fleeting," the queen said, her tone begrudging. "After 1,100 years, even being queen grows tiresome."

I looked up, careful not to meet her eyes. "That is a long time, your majesty."

"Yes. And it's a mere speck of time against all of the eternity I will spend here. But we're not talking about me. I ask you again, what makes you worthy to speak to the Fates?"

My cheeks were hot. "I don't know that I am, but I have to try."

A slight smile flickered across the queen's face. "That is the best answer I've heard yet. Perhaps you will be able to entreat with them after all." She stared at me for a long moment. "Their door has been sealed shut since the time of Hypnos, but perhaps...just perhaps, you could be the key."

"The key?" I asked.

The queen stood, her headdress rattling. "The key to opening the door. After all, you are the first dreamer to enter Urgu in a hundred years. There is something special about that, isn't there?"

"I don't feel special."

The queen stepped down toward me, and then kicked off the ground to hover into the air with her shimmering wings. "I will help you, but first I need a favor."

"What could I have to offer you?"

The queen fluttered nose to nose with me. "Let us examine you, run some tests on your mind and body. For that, I will guide you to the Obsidian Spindle myself."

"What—what kind of tests?"

A voice boomed from the other side of the castle. "The kind you won't wake up from."

I whipped my neck around to see a woman dressed in a red cape, her lips the same red, brandishing two daggers in her hands.

"The Red Rider!" the queen shrieked. "Get her!"

Muirgen pushed up from the ground and joined four other guards who had materialized from nowhere to chase after the Red Rider. She was faster than all of them. One guard, dressed in blue velvet, charged with his lance, and she disarmed him with the flick of her daggers. She threw him into a red-faced pixie, sending them both to the ground.

Another pixie charged from behind, but the Red Rider dodged his attack, backflipping over him then sticking her daggers into his back. The pixie exploded in a hail of glitter. Muirgen was the only one left to fight the Red Rider.

"No!" the queen said. She leaned toward me and muttered, "Watch this. Muirgen is my best fighter."

Muirgen circled the Red Rider for a moment, and then swung her silver sword. The woman dodged the blow and kicked the sword out of Muirgen's hand. It flew across the air and landed inches from where I knelt.

The queen saw an opportunity and grabbed the sword, pointing it at my neck. "ENOUGH!"

"What are you—" I said, but the queen pressed the sword harder against my neck.

"You come for the girl, I presume?"

"There is no reason to parlay with you otherwise," the woman said. "The Unseelie are not worth the air they breathe."

"*Unseelie?*" I said. I pulled at the queen's hands, trying to get the blade away from my skin. "But I thought you were Seelie?"

"We lie!" Muirgen said, inching toward the queen. "That's what we do."

"The Unseelie are unseemly creatures," the Red Rider said. "They look beautiful and kind, but they are truly the most wicked creatures in all of Urgu."

"That depends on your definition of wicked, don't you think?" the queen said.

The Red Rider stomped closer to the throne. "When you are in concert with the Wicked Witch, wicked is part of the job description."

"She is not as wicked as you claim. That was the name given to her by Ozma, bas—"

"Rightful heir to the six provinces of Urgu!"

"Says you!" Muirgen shouted. "Her claim to the throne vanished when Hypnos disappeared, and the line of succession was cut."

"Enough of this," the queen said. "Put down your weapons or I will kill the girl."

"Kill me?" I squeaked.

"You wouldn't," the Red Rider screamed. "You need her."

"No," she said. "There will always be another. In fact, here comes one now. My soldiers have just finished dispatching her."

With that, the door opened, and Chelle was dragged through the door, unconscious, flanked by pixie guards.

"This one smells of Earth, too, and we really only need one for our tests," the queen said with a smirk. "You can't save them both, and yourself at the same time."

The Red Rider held her hands in the air, and then dropped her daggers to the ground. "Fine. You win."

Queen Aine chuckled. "I always do."

CHAPTER 23
CHELLE

I don't know how long I was out, but I woke with a splitting headache. The last thing I remembered was being attacked in the woods. First there were no pixies, then a thousand of them came out of nowhere. There was a bright flash of light, and I was out.

I'd been taken to a small, black cell with only one tiny window offering a slit of light into the room. Across from me was Red, arms folded, tapping her leg against the floor. She was no longer wearing her cape. Her alabaster skin contrasted against her black clothing, though it was so dark I could barely see her red lipstick.

"About time you woke up," she said.

I pushed myself to a seated position. "Sorry for ruining your good time. Where are we?"

"In the queen's dungeon."

"Where's Rose?"

"Being tested on, probably. The queen is desperate for a way out of Urgu, and she and the Wicked Witch are both sure that the answer lies with dreamers like your girlfriend. When they're done with her, and their tests fail, they'll come for us."

I stood up. "We can't let that happen."

"We're not going to. I think I can get us out of here, but first you have to answer something for me."

"What's that?"

"How powerful is your magic?"

"Powerful enough to keep me safe. I only know offensive magic, and a couple of shields, but they are effective."

"Good. The queen is on her way, which means that the magical defenses of this place have been lowered to accommodate her. Can you blow the door?"

I shook my head. "Not if you don't want this whole place to erupt in flames."

"You're right. What about just the doorknob? Can you get it to pop off?"

I scratched my head. "Maybe." I pressed my hand against the cell lock and closed my eyes. "*Incendiarius extitisti.*"

Light from my fingers filled the room. The light turned into heat. I pressed my hand against the lock until it began to sizzle, then it fell off and my hand plunged through the hole in the door. I pushed the door open and turned back to Red.

"What now?"

"Now, we find your girlfriend."

CHAPTER 24
ROSE

No. I didn't like this at all. I mean, I didn't much like being taken away from Chelle and locked in a cage, but I liked it even less when they took me out of the cage and placed wires all over my body.

They brought me into a room that looked like it was straight out of a 1950s sci-fi movie, complete with a bank of knobs and switches on a big metal case along the far wall. Closer to the door, an old computer in a wooden frame blinked green against a black screen. Compared to the rest of Urgu, the room was something out of the distant future, but to a girl from the twenty-first century, it looked like a relic of the past.

"Excuse me?" I asked the gray, shimmerless fairy connecting a suction cup to my left cheek. "What are you doing? I know I keep asking, but I really want to know."

The gray pixie didn't respond. None of them responded to me. It was as if I was speaking a different language. Then I wondered how was it that everybody in Urgu spoke English.

A jet-black fairy covered in dark glitter turned from the computer monitor. "It's because in here all language is translated into whatever you speak. Or I should say, perhaps, that we all speak the same language, but hear it differently."

"Fascinating," I said. "I mean, this whole situation is terrible, but that, at least, is interesting. Another one, though. How can you read my mind?"

"You're connected to my flipperjig, here. I can see everything inside of your brain. Now, I know you have questions," the pixie said, standing up. He didn't have wings like the rest of the pixies, so he walked along the ground. "Unfortunately, I think it's best not to fraternize with the Wicked Witch's test subjects. It's too sad when they don't make it. Scientific objectivity is our first priority."

"Oh. I'm sorry for bumming you out, buddy, but I'm not a lab monkey. If you're gonna kill me, could you please tell me what's going on at least?"

"Well, you are asking so nicely—and honestly, it's not a rule that I'm very good at sticking to. After all, I am so very proud to be a part of the great work of the witch of the east."

"What is it, then?"

The doctor pixie paced back and forth as it talked. "As you are by now no doubt aware, once you enter Urgu, the only way to leave is by death, which is suboptimal, or through the only door which leads back to Earth, behind the Obsidian Spindle."

"I think I knew that. Did I know that?"

"Well, you know it now at least."

"I suppose so."

"And as you are no doubt aware, the Fates have refused to let anyone through the Obsidian Spindle, not since the god Hypnos vanished without a trace."

My heart sank. So much for our great escape plan. "That part I'm pretty sure I didn't know."

"Oh. Well, now you know it, don't you?"

"Yes, I suppose so."

"What you might not know is that we believe there is another way through back to the other side."

"Back to Earth?"

"That's right. You see, there is a barrier that separates this world from Earth, and from the rest of the universe. It is incredibly powerful and incredibly stable. However, it, like everything else in Urgu, is powered by dreams, and since Hypnos's disappearance, there have been no more dreams. That makes the barrier weak." The pixie hurried in his pacing, lost in scientific permutations. "We think, if we direct a charge—a dreamer's soul—at the perfect frequency and it hits the barrier, we can puncture the barrier and return to Earth."

I blinked. "And what? You think I have that frequency?"

He stopped pacing and looked at me. "Well, I'm not sure yet. However, you did just come through the field and into Urgu. Chances are, there's some sort of residue on you which could give us a key to the frequency."

"And what happens to Urgu when the barrier falls?"

The pixie smiled. "It's not what happens to Urgu that is important, my dear. It's what happens to Earth. People cannot survive without dreams, but we can. While the dreamless world devolves into madness, we will make our strike. We will take over the earth."

"That's crazy."

"No!" The pixie snarled, baring his jagged teeth at me. "What's crazy is being stuck here for generation after generation with nothing to do but plot our escape. The Fates could let us go, but instead, they choose to stay cooped up behind their hydra, bound inside their onyx tower, and force our hands."

"Maybe they have their reasons."

"Maybe," the pixie said, settling down and giving a shrug. "But we don't care about them, now do we?"

"I do! You're going to turn everybody on Earth mad!"

"Only a little. Don't worry, they'll still have nightmares after all. Although, you won't have to worry about that."

"So, you're going to kill me then?" I asked, trying to stay brave. I was still mostly dead, after all. Still, I couldn't keep my bottom lip from quivering.

"Yes," the pixie said. "You truly are remarkable, you know. Your soul resonated at the perfect frequency to penetrate the barrier to Urgu, a feat that has not been accomplished in a hundred years. I believe that means you can become a conduit between Earth and this place. I have tested my theory on hundreds of dreamers over the years, but they were old souls by the time our tests began and had no body back on Earth waiting for them. Unfortunately, it didn't work—"

"Because they had been dead for a long time?"

"Precisely, but you are different. You are fresh, and thus, have a body waiting for you."

"And what if I don't? What if my body is dead, too?"

"Let's not think like that," the pixie said with a smile. "Positive energy. Because you see, it is your connection to your body that makes you so special. We hope to use that connection to establish a link back to Earth and use it like a sword to cut the barrier in twain. The process will kill you, but free us. You will be a hero to our people."

"I don't want to be a hero."

"Too bad. I did not want to end up here, but we play the cards we are dealt, yes?" The doctor played with the dials on the ancient, wooden computer. "You're going to feel a slight pinch. I would like to say it gets better, but it doesn't. That pinch will become a dull ache, then a throb, next comes a piercing migraine, and eventually you will vibrate so fast that you explode. Hopefully, by then, you will have helped us locate what we need."

"No, thank you," I said. "I'd rather not."

The pixie stood next to a giant lever. He wrapped his hand around the knob. "I'm afraid you don't have much of a choice." Without another word, he flipped the lever, and the pain began.

At first, he was right. It didn't hurt too bad, but soon it was excruciating enough that a scream emerged—despite me, without my permission—from the depths of my soul. I tried to focus. I tried to think. I tried to remember Chelle, and how much I loved her.

I needed to stay alive for her, but a few moments later the pain was so great I couldn't think of anything else, and that's when I knew I was going to die.

CHAPTER 25
RED

"Be quiet," I growled at the gorgon clomping behind me. "Can you do that?"

"Yes," she snapped. She took her cloak hung up outside the cell and tossed it over her back. "You don't have to condescend to me. I can handle myself."

"Can you? I've only known you a day. In that time, I managed to get the drop on you, and then you were captured by pixies. I'm surprised you've lived this long. Now, be quiet."

Pixies were arrogant and brash. They didn't believe prisoners could escape from their cells, which is how I'd escaped a half dozen times in a half dozen ways. They had especially low opinions of humans.

There were few guards inside the castle. The pixies preferred to place guards around the forest than in the castle itself, as the forest was very large and they were very small, so it took a lot of them to cover the whole forest.

If they hadn't killed or captured every one of their Seelie cousins, then perhaps they could have guarded the forest from others together, but Unseelie didn't like to share, and they definitely didn't think to the future.

"Where are we going?" Chelle said.

I spoke to her over my shoulder, my voice a low murmur. "The laboratories are on the other side of the throne room from us, and if you aren't quiet, we're going to be discovered before we get there."

"My queen."

I was standing outside the throne room and still I could recognize the muffled voice. The Wicked Witch had reported to the castle.

The two pixies guarding the door left their posts and walked toward the queen when the witch arrived. Nobody trusted the evil witch, not even her closest allies.

I peered around the door jamb and saw her standing in front of the throne, dressed in a flowing black gown which shimmered as brightly as the pixie queen. It was subtle enough that only the deftest eye could tell it was on purpose. Nobody shined brighter than the witch.

"Nimue," Aine said dully, strumming her fingers on her golden throne. "To what do I owe the pleasure of your company?"

Nimue's cold blue eyes were the only part of her that wasn't made up to look black. She wore dark black eyeshadow and lipstick and enchanted her hair to an onyx black from its normal strawberry blond. She wore a crown of black roses, and a necklace made from melted obsidian. The key around her neck was just as black, glaring against her light white skin.

Nimue stared at Aine, careful to impose her will on the pixie queen and prove she was more powerful. "Let us not split hairs, Aine. No one has been pleased by my company in decades, and neither are you, now. I'm here for the girl. The one you captured."

"She is my prisoner," the queen said, her voice hard. "You may have gained the right to rule Oz, but here you have no power to command anything."

When the witch smiled, her black lipstick parted to reveal the gleaming white teeth underneath. "We are great allies, my queen. I would never presume to demand anything from you. Rather, it is a great favor to me, if you would part with her."

"She is part of the grand experiment. One you designed yourself. You can have her once we're done with her."

"She'll be dead when you're done."

"Only if you're wrong and she is not the key to piercing the barrier. If you're right, she might still live, and we will have unlocked a great power. Perhaps the greatest power in the universe."

"And that is what you want, isn't it? Great power?"

Aine flew into the air. "What I want is the power to go home, back to Earth. That is what we're all working for, every one of us, and the only reason we would agree to work with the likes of you."

The witch snapped her fingers, and fire appeared in her hand. "You will give her to me, or I will burn your precious forest to the ground."

"Guards!" the pixie queen screamed. "Do that, and you will not make it out of here alive. Your parlor tricks are no match for pixie magic."

The deadly standoff lasted several tense moments before Nimue laughed and the fire in her hand disappeared. "Look at us, in a pissing match like a couple of kings. Are we not better than this?"

Aine nodded slightly. "I am, at least."

A guttural scream echoed down the passage on the other side of the throne room—in the direction of the laboratories. It was the dreamer, the girl Rose. From behind me, the gorgon left her place and ran forward. "Rose!"

Chelle darted into the throne room without any thought to her welfare, or mine, and I had no choice but to follow her. She was going to be the death of me, if I didn't kill her first.

CHAPTER 26

CHELLE

I knew it was stupid to run into the throne room the minute that I did it, but that didn't stop my legs from churning. Red cursed at me under her breath as I moved past her, but soon enough she was behind me.

"Where are we going?" I shouted as Red overtook me and bolted ahead.

"You're going to get us both killed, or worse!"

"I don't care! That's Rose screaming and I'm not going to let her suffer!"

We were halfway through the hall when the pixies turned to us. Their queen let out a horrible squeal. "Get them!"

Two pixie guards flew toward us, and I extended my arms. Red had told me that the magic around the castle would prevent me from using my own, but it had already worked once, so I had to try again.

"Close your eyes!"

Red threw up her hands. "Are you crazy? How am I gonna see?"

"Just do it!" I shouted. "*Mico a lumen!*"

A flash of light filled the room, and Red and I disappeared down the hallway where I'd heard Rose screaming.

"*Fulminis!*" I shouted. Another flash of lightning flew from my hands and crashed onto the archway that led to the throne room, sending it crashing to the ground.

"Hopefully that will buy us some time," Red said. "It's just up ahead."

She didn't have to tell me that, because Rose's shrieks grew louder the closer we came to the end of the hallway. Bright blue light emanated from the room, and when I got close enough, I could see her strapped to a hospital bed, blue currents running toward her.

Red smashed into the room and hurled daggers through the necks of two guards standing against the near wall.

"What the—" A bespectacled black pixie stood up from the front of what looked like a wooden computer screen.

Red picked him up by the collar. "Turn it off!"

"I can't!" the pixie said, trying to break free. "Once it's started, only death or success can stop it!"

"Screw this!" I screamed. "*Fulminis!*"

The lightning crashed out of my fingers and toward the big computer terminal next to Rose. The surge of electricity caused an explosion on the board, and the entire computer terminal sizzled and crackled before going silent.

"You've ruined everything!" the pixie said. "It was working!"

Red twisted the doctor's neck around, and he fell limply to the floor. I ran over to Rose and unlatched her from the harness.

"Wake up!" I said but got no response. "Wake up!"

I started to cry, but Red placed her hand on my shoulder. "She's not dead. She would have turned to dust if she was dead. We'll wake her. I promise. We have to get out of here first, though. Drink this."

Red handed me a red potion before downing one herself. I uncapped the bottle and drank it. My stomach felt queasy for a moment, and then I shot toward the ceiling like a rocket. In an instant, we had regained our previous size and broken through the roof of the castle.

I looked over at Red, who had Rose clutched tightly in her hands. "Come on. We have to get out of here. We just became the number one enemy on the Unseelie's hit list."

CHAPTER 27

NIMUE

"Break it down!" I shouted at the pixies as they struggled to move the hefty debris blocking our way to the laboratory.

The gorgon wasn't supposed to be able to do that. Nobody was supposed to be able to use magic in Urgu. Nobody except for me and the pixies. I only had power because I had given myself, mind and soul, to the great god Hera. In return, she bestowed upon me the divine right to use magic.

It was the reason monsters didn't have much respect for me. They had all the magic they wanted, but we humans were just supposed to live in the dirt and worship them. I didn't think so.

"Out of my way!" I screamed. "Repair!"

The rocks moved out of the way, and back to their original location. Most magic casters thought the original Latin was important to the spell, but the spell worked just as well in any language. It was the aptitude of the caster and her conviction in the words that mattered.

"Get them!" the queen shouted.

The guards flew forward in a hesitant, nervous rush, and they had every reason to be scared. Pixies who disappointed Aine were subject to her wrath, and that was bad enough when I wasn't in the castle. When I was here, everybody was uneasy, even the queen. They didn't much like me, but they could not deny the power of Hera. Aine had no interest in disappointing Hera and bringing Hera's wrath down on them. After all, her vengeance was legendary.

I followed behind the pixies, slowly. There was no reason for a queen to interfere with a battle. My job was more political and diplomatic. I wasn't here for hacking somebody to pieces or frying them alive. There were certainly moments for that, and they were not without their satisfaction. I quite enjoyed the sizzle of a freshly fried dissident.

I reached the end of the hallway just as a large brown shoe exploded through the door. The pixies flew past me, and I didn't need to stay to find out what had happened.

"Away!" I shouted, and I vanished in a puff of smoke.

I reappeared outside the castle, which was little more than a smoking heap, as two figures rushed off into the woods.

"Enlarge!" I screamed, and I returned my normal height. I didn't need potions or tricks to change my size and shape, but that's because I was the most powerful magician in Urgu. Even a spell-casting gorgon could not rival that power.

I needed to learn more about the magic-wielder who had just destroyed Queen Aine's castle. I looked down at the pink ruin, crumbling to bits, and it was hard not to smile. For appearance's sake, I would make sure to denounce the escapees as criminals, but it was hard not to believe that Aine got what she deserved for underestimating humanity.

Of course, I hoped she would continue to do so until I was rid of her forever.

CHAPTER 28

ROSE

How long had I been out? The last thing I remembered was being shocked with lightning, certain I was about to die, and I'd woken up in some sort of cave, across a fire from a woman in dark clothes and a red cape. And there was my darling Chelle, staring into the flames, lost in silence.

"What happened?" I asked groggily, sitting up from the dirt which had been my bed.

"You're up!" Chelle said. She ran over and hugged me tightly. "I thought we had lost you."

"I knew we hadn't," the woman wearing a long, flowing, red cape said. "Welcome back, Rose."

"Who are you?" I asked.

"You can call me Red. I think that is the preferred nomenclature of your friend here, and I quite like it, too."

Chelle kissed my cheek, and then my lips. "I'm so happy you're awake. How do you feel?"

"Fine." I stroked my face where she had kissed me. "Where are we? How did we get here?"

The Red Rider stood. "We're in a cave, obviously. As for where we are, I don't think it would be of any interest to you. Just know we're on a path to the Obsidian Spindle."

"That's good news," I said, turning to Chelle. "Isn't that good news?"

Chelle leaned back. "No. Not really. Getting to the Obsidian Spindle is going to be harder than we thought."

"Well, I already thought it was going to be really hard. How much harder could it possibly be?"

"There are only two ways to the Obsidian Spindle. One is to cross the dangerous Cursed Sea, full of monsters of the deep, and the other is through the throne room—the Wicked Witch's throne room, right in the heart of Oz."

"That doesn't sound too bad."

Chelle gulped. "There's more."

"Of course there is."

"The castle is guarded by hundreds of troops and enchantments," Red said. "And Hera is always watching. When Ozma ruled the throne, she would have helped us. She was kind to the Fates, and in turn they opened their doors to her. The Wicked Witch is not so kind. Even if we make it through the throne room against the will of Hera, the spindle is guarded by a seven-headed hydra which bends only to the rightful heir's will."

"Then we'll go across the sea," I replied. "That sounds like an easy choice."

"That would be easier, but not by much. There is another option, though."

"You're not going to like this," Chelle muttered.

"Help us bring Ozma back to the throne," the Red Rider said. "Help us right the wrong that Nimue brought about, and then we can go to the Obsidian Spindle together, with Ozma's blessing."

"Like I told you," Chelle said. "We can't do that. We have to get to the Spindle before Rose's body gives out. We don't have time to fight your wars."

Red came over to me and knelt by my side. "This is about more than just you. There hasn't been another dreamer in Urgu in a hundred years. I believe you may be the secret to stopping Hera and bringing peace to our land. More than that, I believe you could bring dreamers back to this world and tip the balance of sanity in yours."

"Excuse me," Chelle said. "I made it here, too."

"Yes, yes," The Red Rider said. "But you didn't come here like Rose did. She is the key."

"I—I can't," I said after a long moment. "This has been fun, but I'm no action hero. Look at me. I've been here one day and already almost died multiple times. It's safer if I just go home."

"And damn all of Urgu in the process?"

Chelle nodded. "That's right."

The Red Rider stood. "That is disappointing. I thought you were made of sterner stuff."

"I don't know why," I said, scratching my head. "You only just met me, and I've been unconscious until just now."

The Red Rider turned to me. "Will you at least meet Ozma, and tell her to her face that you are a coward?"

"Hey!" Chelle said. "She's not a coward. We just want to go home. This isn't our war."

"It's everybody's war!" Red was nearly shouting. "If you leave, you will doom not only us, but all of humanity as well."

"Screw humanity," Chelle said. "What have they ever done for me?"

"I'm a human." I lowered my eyes to the ground.

Chelle turned to me. "Not you, though. You're one of the good ones."

"And you don't think there are more good ones back on Earth? I'm sorry, but...I do."

"I'm sure there are," Chelle said, "but we don't have to go risking our lives for them."

"I would hope somebody would risk their life for me." I gulped loudly. "Very well. I will meet your queen and tell her to her face that I will not help."

"She's just trying to guilt you," Chelle said.

"I know," I said, nodding. "However, I owe it to the universe, I suppose, to explain myself to this Ozma. I mean, can you believe Ozma is real? I used to read about her in stories. Look at this. A red rider just like Little Red Riding Hood. I mean, do you not want to meet her?"

"I don't really care!"

"Really? Honestly, that's kind of weird."

"I never read fairy tales. I had my own monsters to deal with."

"Still, it's some kind of coincidence."

"It's not a coincidence," the Red Rider said. "The Dream Realm seeps into every human on the planet. We here in this realm become the dreams for you on Earth."

"That's not what Ursa told me," I replied. "She said that humans created the things in the Dream Realm."

"Who's Ursa?" Red said, confused.

"My bear friend."

"A bear?" Red chuckled. "You're going to trust a bear?"

My eyes drifted to the floor. "She was nice to me."

"I'm sure she was, but she was also...a bear. Still, she's not entirely wrong. The truth is that dreams are a two-way street. Yes, sometimes humans create things here, but more often than not, the things we created here get stolen by humans and used in their stories. For instance, have you heard of Oz?"

I nodded. "Of course. There's like a thousand books and bunch of movies."

"It is the greatest city in Urgu, forged by Hypnos himself to protect the Obsidian Spindle, and constructed more than ten thousand years ago. When the rightful ruler ascended to the throne, she took the name of the city as a tribute to Hypnos and the greatest city in all of Urgu."

"Whoa," Chelle said, and I agreed with the sentiment, even if all I did was smile at Red.

"The great city of Oz, also known as the Emerald City, is one of those things that seeped into your world, and there are hundreds, thousands more. Dreamers come and they see things in their dreams. Over centuries and generations dreams become memories and memories become ideas. Then, ideas are written into stories."

"Why does it have two names?" Chelle asked, and I thought it a very good question, though not the one I would have asked.

"I don't know, it just does. Don't cities have two names back on Earth?"

"Like New York City and the Big Apple?" Chelle asked.

"Sure. If that is true, then yes exactly that. It probably also has something to do with Oz being the name of the city and the Land of Oz is the name of this province of Urgu."

"Yup," Chelle nodded. "Definitely like New York City then. New York is the city and the state."

"Wonderful," Red replied, rolling her eyes. "This has been truly fascinating. Can we move on now?"

"So everything in our dreams is true?" I asked. "All our ideas come from here?"

"Not all of it, but some of it. Ideas happen other ways. The muses work with many instruments. However, some of it comes from here as well."

"That's pretty cool." I looked at Chelle. "I mean, this whole thing sucks, but that is pretty cool. Isn't it, Chelle?"

She shook her head. "It's fine, I guess. I just want to get you home."

"We'll go there, but maybe we'll have an adventure along the way."

"Adventurous get people killed," Chelle said.

I couldn't argue with her, but for once in my life, I was the one who was the subject of an adventure, and not Chelle. I hadn't even known I wanted adventure until that moment, and the thought of it turned my stomach, but I liked the feeling of doing something like I'd always read about in stories.

The Red Rider looked at Chelle. "Do you have a way to conceal yourself? The people of Urgu do not like monsters. If they find us on the road, they will not like it."

Chelle pulled an amulet out of her pocket. She placed it over her head. As she did, the gorgon I fell in love with disappeared, replaced by a beautiful, black women with nappy, wild hair and a bright, white smile. She looked over at me.

"How do I look?" Chelle asked.

I smiled. "Same as you always do. Beautiful."

CHAPTER 29

NIMUE

One of the advantages of being a witch was the ability to travel to wherever you wanted to be whenever you wanted to be there. Moments before, I had been inside the woods, staring down the rubble of the pixie queen's castle, and now I was back in the emerald castle which I had called home for a hundred years as queen, and several hundred as royal advisor to the crown.

One hundred years? Had it really been so long since I sold myself to the goddess Hera and took the throne from that brat queen?

The disappearance of Hypnos gave us an opening, but it was I that carried out the sacking of Oz and the removal of Ozma. She played at being just a child, but she was hundreds of years old when I met her. I saw right through her pomp to the vain woman she truly was. Imagine, being so vain as to claim the name of Oz when you ascended to the throne.

"Nimue." I heard the whisper in my bedchamber. It was my god, my Hera.

"Yes, your majesty," I said, dropping to the ground. There were none I feared in Urgu except for her. With her blessing, I could carry out incredible acts. Without her, I would be powerless, like the worm I was before we met.

Two purple eyes materialized in the darkness. "Did you find the girl?"

I took a deep breath in. Though she knew the answer, she wanted me to admit it. It was the same form of power I held over my subjects, and I had learned from her. "No, your majesty."

"Pitiful. To think I chose you above all others to carry out my bidding."

"I'm sorry, your grace. I will find them."

"I know you will," my goddess said. "You have grown too accustomed to your power to risk losing it now...not when we are so close. That girl is the one we need to finally break free of this place, and when we are free, I will control the universe, and you will rule by my side."

"Yes, my goddess. I will do everything in my power to make that happen."

"See that your power doesn't fail me," Hera replied. "Or, I will see to it that it runs out, and I will choose another to touch with my countenance."

Her eyes faded into the darkness and she was gone from the room before I stood. Her absence left me with the empty feeling of dread that had accompanied every one of our encounters for the whole of the last century.

CHAPTER 30

RED

"Let's go!" I shouted back to Chelle and Rose.

The Queen's Road led through the forest and into the Emerald City itself. We had been traveling on it for less than an hour and already they were lagging behind. I worried that we would be caught by the Wicked Witch's guards, but it was still the quickest way to Ozma. We were through the worst of the forest, but its trees still lined the way for another five miles. It would take all day to move through this, if Rose and Chelle didn't hurry.

"I'm trying," Rose replied. "I just didn't think it would be this much walking. I mean, this is a dream. Can't we just teleport there?"

I sighed. "That's not how it works here."

Rose didn't seem that interesting or important to me, except that she was the first person to make it through the barrier in a century. If it wasn't for that, she would be completely ordinary.

And yet, I watched how she interacted with her gorgon girlfriend, Chelle. There was nothing like that when I was alive. Monsters and humans lived completely separately and at odds with each other. Even when there were alliances, they were shaky at best and often disbanded in bloodshed.

Rose didn't have any of that contempt for monsters. She held hands with Chelle freely and openly, as if it was the most normal thing in the world. Perhaps things had changed on Earth in the last hundred years, because even those that made it here before the disappearance of Hypnos did not treat monsters well. Still, I was happy she agreed to wear the amulet which covered her gorgon appearance.

"Can't we just take a wagon," Rose said. "Like that one."

I looked back on the road in a panic. There shouldn't be a wagon on the road. Not yet. The road through the forest was too treacherous for any but the queen's soldiers to traverse, and I had tracked the schedule of the Queen's Guard before I left for Critterton. No envoy was supposed to be on the road for a week.

But Rose was right. A wooden carriage pulled by a pair of oxen came into view from around the tree line.

"Get down!" I shouted, rushing toward a ditch at the side of the road. I jumped inside. In a moment Chelle and Rose joined me.

"What are we hiding from?" Chelle asked, inching closer to me.

I peeked my head out of the ditch. I feared the wagon was from Oz. Sure enough, emerald banners hung from its roof. There must have been an emergency that caused the queen to move up her next shipment of dreams.

Dreams were mined from the center of Urgu, and every year we were forced to mine closer and closer to the core, and our supply of dreams grew scarce. It was dangerous work, and only the dwarves could handle that kind of heat in that kind of depth. Once they were mined, the queen controlled the supply, distributing them on her whim. Ozma distributed the dreams equally and fairly, but Nimue... she used dreams to reward her sycophants.

"It's the royal dream changer. There will be a half dozen royal guards not far behind."

The ground thundered beneath me. From the distance, a cadre of knights on horseback, replete with emerald plate armor and carrying the banners of the Witched Witch, came around the corner.

"Stay quiet," I said, slouching down against the ground.

Dreams did more than simply power Urgu. They were its currency as well. Dreams could be exchanged for anything, and the more powerful the dream, the more it was worth. Since there had been no new dreams in a hundred years, they were a precious commodity, and worth killing over.

The thunderous vibrations quickened and grew more intense, until the shadow of the carriage and the knights fell over us, and then passed by. They had not seen us. Good.

The dream changer oversaw the distribution of dreams throughout the kingdom and was thus the second most powerful human in all of Urgu, after the queen. As such, she had the most elite knights in all of Urgu, as she kept the currency for the kingdom, and was an easy target for thieves.

I poked my head up one more time to watch them clomp away. Then, something unexpected happened. A hail of arrows launched into the air from the far tree line and arched onto the road. The arrows embedded into several of the knights and forced the horses to buck. One knight fell to the ground near me and evaporated from view; his ashes could be seen on the wind.

"Attack!" A loud yell came from the trees, and a group of poorly dressed men and women, most with flaming red hair, flooded onto the road from either side and engaged the knights in hand to hand combat. They carried swords, clubs, and mallets.

Even with arrows riddling the knights' armor, there was little hope for the attackers. I turned back to Chelle and gestured to Rose. "Stay here and protect her!"

I pulled myself onto the road and charged. Close combat was not my strength, but I couldn't let the attackers be killed. Any enemy of the Wicked Witch was a friend to me.

I leapt onto the back of one of the horses and stuck a knight in the neck as she readied for attack. I kicked her to the ground and lunged at another. This one I tackled to the ground. As the horse bucked into the air, I rolled away and the full weight of the horse came crashing down onto the knight, evaporating him instantly.

I pushed myself back to my feet to attack again, but the rest of the group had slain the other knights, and one of them with dirty brown clothes and flaming red hair walked toward the carriage of the dream changer.

I snuck closer to hear what their leader said.

"It's not a very good day for you, is it, Cordelia?"

A bald woman with fat cheeks and a tall green hat poked her head out of the carriage. "Nimue will not be happy."

"She's never happy," the woman said. "Now, pay up."

The fat woman smiled. "I think not. You see, you're very predictable, Diedre. I think very much that you will be the one paying up today."

"What do you mean?"

The shriek echoed through the tree moments before I saw the wings of the demon dragon known as Bastonel, clad in bright silver armor like a knight, and blowing a thick barrage of fire into the air.

"Oh, no." I took off running. "It's the great dragon, Bastonel. Let's go!"

I leapt down into the ditch and headed for the tree line, pulling Rose along with me. The forest was a slower route than the Queen's Road, but they would get us there in shadow. I stupidly traded speed for stealth, and it might have gotten us killed.

"What about those people?" Rose asked as we ran.

"They're all going to die," I replied. "It's the price we all pay when we go against the queen, sooner or later."

"No!" Rose said. "Chelle, you can't let them die. Please, Chelle."

"They're not my concern," Chelle said. "You're my only concern."

"If what Red told us is true, then we all have to help fight the queen. All of us. Even them, and even you."

"Grrrr!" Chelle screamed. "You are so annoying. Go. I will catch up."

"Are you sure?" I asked.

Chelle nodded. "You hurt her, and I will end you."

"There's a town up ahead. Meet us at Happy Dragon Inn in K'dech."

Chelle nodded. "I'll see you there."

I couldn't wait another second. The dragon was about to attack, and I had to get Rose to safety. I turned away and disappeared into the brush with the dreamer.

CHAPTER 31
CHELLE

"Obice glacies praesidium!"

A flood of ice poured out of my hand as I jetted toward the carriage. The fighters were huddled, ready to fight, ready to die. The dragon blew firey breath at them, but my ice reached its target and created a barrier between them and the dragon.

"Run!" I shouted.

The fire was hot, and it melted the ice quickly. I kept pouring new ice into the barrier as the fighters ran backwards away from the blast. I was as strong as I had ever been, but Bastonel was made of fire and kept burning through all but the thinnest vale of my ice barrier.

I was tiring out quickly. It took quite a bit of willpower to cast an ice shield, especially one so big. With my gorgon lineage, I was able to draw from a deeper well than most humans, but even I couldn't keep the barrier up forever.

"Go!" I shouted to the last few fighters remaining.

"We can't leave the dreams!" one of them shouted back. "They're desperately needed to buy food and clothing."

"Then hurry up and get it! You're about to be charred and then none of that will matter."

Bastonel was right on top of my barrier now. He reared up on his hind legs and crashed his front claws down upon it. The pressure dropped me to the ground. My hands began to shake, and I gritted my teeth, biting down on my cheek to keep conscious.

The dragon was too much.

I collapsed to the ground and with me, the ice barrier fell. Bastonel landed with either claw next to my head. I felt the heat of his breath even though there was no fire to go with it. Even just a simple inhale felt like being stuck into a bonfire, face first.

He reared back a second time, ready to char me alive, and while he was in the air I rolled under his belly.

"Moles glaciei in spica!"

A huge geyser of water came from my hands and froze, forming a five-foot-tall spike, which I pushed deep into the dragon's stomach. Bastonel screamed out in pain as his blood melted the ice and dripped down onto my face. The fire lizard writhed in agony and collapsed next to me on the ground. Dead.

"You did it!" It was the red-haired woman who led the charge.

"I did," I said, stumbling toward the forest, back to where I'd left Rose.

"You can't go off now," the woman said, watching me. "Look at you. You're—"

That was the last word I heard before collapsing into her arms, completely spent. I had never used that much magic before, and never so quickly. As I felt the consciousness fade from me, I wondered if it would hurt when I evaporated into thin air.

CHAPTER 32
ROSE

"It's been too long," I said, turning around and heading back towards where we'd left Chelle.

Red caught up with me and put a hand on my shoulder. "She's fighting a dragon. It's not too long."

"Oh my god. I asked her to fight a dragon!" I broke free of Red's grasp. "Why would I tell her to fight a dragon? What kind of girlfriend does that?"

There was a long silence. "A bad one."

"What!" I shouted. "You just said she's going to be fine."

"All right, you caught me. I have no idea if she's going to be fine. I don't know her. She seems like a fighter though. Is she a fighter?"

I smiled. "Yeah, she's a fighter."

"Then she's got a better shot than most. Do you trust her?"

"Of course I trust her. I don't trust the dragon."

"I can't fight a dragon, Rose. Neither can you. The only person who stands a shot is Chelle, because she's a monster, too."

"She's not a monster!"

"Whoa, easy, tiger. I wasn't saying it to offend. I meant she has magic flowing through her, like a dragon does. The best thing we can do is get to the Happy Dragon and wait for her."

"What if she doesn't come?"

There was another long moment. "She'll come."

"And what if she doesn't?"

Red looked me in the eyes. "Do you really want to have that conversation now?"

I gulped. "I really don't."

Red held out her hand. "Then let's go."

I looked back one last time through the trees, hoping that Chelle would come back out and tell me everything was okay, but it was only a pipe dream. I had doomed the love of my life, really the only thing in the world that I loved, to near certain death.

CHAPTER 33
CHELLE

I rested for the rest of the evening on a bed of hay. By the next morning, I regained my strength. I picked myself up and walked out of the thatched-roof hut to find a little village. The houses were all made from mud and covered in the same kind of hay that I rested on in my infirmed condition. There were no paved roads in the little town, just dirt, but the people passing by looked happy enough, even if they were a little dusty. A couple sat over a black kettle as it cooked, while children ran around and played with sticks, rocks, and kites.

"Over here," I heard from behind me. It was the red-haired woman, now with a much thicker Irish accent than I remembered her having in the woods. She was sitting under a tree sewing a bag.

I walked over to her. The wind was light against my skin, and the air smelled of fresh grass. I hadn't noticed the smell the whole time I was in Urgu, but for some reason, in that moment, every scent felt more vibrant.

"This is a far cry from fighting," I said, sitting down.

"Fightin's not all we do. It's just a piece of what we do, when we have to." She glanced at me, then focused again on her work, pulling the needle through the burlap. "You use magic. Not many people here can use magic."

"I'm not most people."

"Yes, I'm aware of that." She placed the half-finished bag down and looked at me. "What god do you serve then?"

I chuckled. "I don't serve a god."

She leaned in and whispered hoarsely, a knowing smile on her face. "I don't believe you. The only ones who can use magic here gave their souls to one of the gods trapped in this place."

"Like Hypnos or Hera?"

She nodded. "That's two of them, except Hypnos isn't trapped here. He's here by choice. This is his domain."

"And he's lost."

"Aye, that too."

"What other gods are there?"

The woman used her finger to draw what looked like a kidney bean on the ground. Above the concave part of the bean, she drew a little circle.

"Up here," she said, pointing to the circle. "That's the Obsidian Spindle. The most powerful object in Urgu, maybe the whole universe."

I nodded. "I've heard of it."

"Good. Back before the universe existed, there was nothing but darkness."

"We can skip that part, I think."

"Fair enough. But you should know that for a time, this land didn't exist. It wasn't until Zeus gave humanity the spark of life, that this place was created."

"Why then?"

"Because while we are all born with the spark inside of us, our bodies are too brittle to handle it. The charge keeps building up, and we needed a place to disperse it."

"Like a battery."

"I dunno what that is, but...sure. If that helps you, then yes.

That's when Hera decided that dreams would be the perfect place to keep the excess energy. The gods created the Sleep Realm and granted Nox, goddess of Darkness, dominion over everything there. In turn, Nox broke this land in half, into the Dream Realm, and the Nightmare Realm. She gave control of the Dream Realm, this realm, to her son Hypnos, and the Nightmare Realm to her son Epiales."

"I've been there, it sucks."

"It is home to the most fearsome things in the universe. If Nox had not separated them, then the Nightmare Realm would have overrun this place eons ago. The fact that you survived being there says a lot about you."

"Well, I had help from my mother," I replied. "But this doesn't explain anything about what's going on here, or the gods trapped here."

"I'm getting there. I'm getting there. I'm sorry. I get lost in my own stories, but I promise I'm getting there."

"Fine."

"So, in the beginning, there was only Hypnos in this realm, y'see? He bent this place to his will and created the continent of Urgu. For a time, things were good, though he was lonely. That's why he allowed humanity to settle on Urgu—certain parts of humanity, at least. Those without bodies and those without consciousnesses."

"Right. People in a coma and people who died in their sleep."

"The gods would not allow him to take everybody, but they granted him some leeway as to those who were allowed to inhabit his land. Again, things thrived."

I pressed the bridge of my nose with my hand. "I'm on my last nerve with this story."

"You have no respect for the art of narrative."

"I'm a product of my generation. We like things quick and easy. Unfortunately, I have a feeling there's not a Wikipedia entry about this."

"I don't know what that is."

"I know. Just keep going."

"Over the centuries, Urgu thrived, even though it was cut off from the outside world."

"Why was it cut off?"

"Ah, see. I would have told you if you didn't force me to go faster."

"You got me there."

"It was cut off because the realm of dreams cannot cross over to the realm of man. The dreams we store here, the ones that power everything, are volatile and unstable to humanity. If anything were to happen, and the dreams were to reenter the world, well, humanity would...it would not be good."

"Explosions or something? People exploding with too much of the god particle?"

"We don't know for sure, but yes, we assume something like that. That's why the Dream Realm and the Nightmare Realm are cut off from the outside world through barriers which lock them away from the rest of the universe. And it's why they make excellent prisons."

"Prisons?"

"For the only type of being that cannot be imprisoned anywhere else."

"Gods."

"Exactly."

"Epiales refused to act as a jailer, but Hypnos, the ever-dutiful son, accepted the burden." The woman drew a line down the center of the bean. "First, it was Hera. She and Hypnos battled for control of Urgu, and eventually split the land in half."

The woman drew a line from the middle to the right side. She pointed to the top left. "Then, Loki, trickster god." She pointed to the top right of the map. "Agrona, goddess of slaughter." Then she drew a second line down the middle. "Eventually, Hera and Hypnos were relegated to the middle of the land, closest to the Obsidian Spindle, with Hypnos in control of the island that housed the Obsidian Spindle, and the bridge which spanned between it and the mainland.

This was where he set up his great city, Oz, and blocked Hera's minions from his land by the Great Wall."

"Why were they locked into the middle?" I asked.

She pointed to the bottom right. "Because Sekhmet was sent here, and needed a place to rule, so Hypnos ceded some of his land to her." She pointed to the bottom left. "And so was Anansi, which meant Hypnos lost more and more. He is a kind god, but Hypnos is not a warrior. He could not fight six gods. Six gods vying for the same land, which is why I ask you: What god do you serve?"

I looked at her. "What god do you serve?"

"I don't serve any, thus why I am destined for a life of poverty. I do have an affinity for Agrona, though, being a Celt myself."

"And who are you, exactly?"

"They called me Deidre in my old life." She shook her head and shifted her eyes to the ground. "The woman who started a war because she pursued the love of her life and humiliated a king."

"What happened to him?"

Diedre sighed. "He died in battle, not in his sleep, so I'll never see him again."

"That sucks," I said after a long silence. I was never good at emotion, but I knew enough to understand that to get Diedre to help me, I needed her to like me. "My girlfriend, the love of my life, fell into a coma, and I came here to save her. That's why I can use magic. I'm not from here. I didn't wake up here. I'm just here. But you are from here, so maybe you can help me."

Diedre stared at me for a moment, sizing me up. "I've already done my bit for you, but I will try to do more if I can."

"Do you know the Happy Dragon Inn?"

Diedre nodded. "I've heard of it. It's not far from here."

"Can you take me to it?"

She nodded again. "Of course, but I was hoping you'd help me first."

My eyes narrowed at her. "Help you do what?"

A wry smile crossed her lips. "A job that is particularly suited for your expertise. The Wicked Witch has a group of my men held prisoner. They are being guarded by a giant. We can't fight it alone, but with your help, we stand a fighting shot."

I stood up. "No way, I almost died once today. That's enough."

"Fine. I guess you could find that inn on your own."

"Are you kidding?" I asked, flailing my arms in frustration. "I saved your life on the road earlier. Or don't you remember when I fought that dragon?"

She stood. "And we saved yours. Now, a favor for a favor. Help us, and we'll bring you to your beloved. I swear it by the old gods."

I snorted. If I could have breathed fire, I would have, but instead I just snarled at her. "Fine. But I don't have to like it."

She shook her head. "No, you don't. You just have to do it."

CHAPTER 34

RED

The city of K'dech sat at the mouth of the Willick mountain range and was the last stop on the Queen's Road before travelers reached Oz. The city was ancient a thousand years before and had changed hands so many times it boasted a combination of ancient Mayan, Chinese, and Greek architecture.

Back when dreamers still came to Urgu, K'dech was often the first major city they came to on their trek to Oz, and everybody trekked to Oz at some point. An old Muslim man once told me about travelling toward Mecca and the call deep in his bones, all his life, to journey there. He hoped one day he would get to complete his pilgrimage, but died in his sleep, and ended up in Urgu. However, he said that the call of the Emerald City was just as great.

I felt no great calling to enter Oz when I first walked there from the Sandlands so many centuries ago. I came for the same reason as everyone else, to visit the Obsidian Spindle and seek the council of the Fates, but it was not some religious experience. It was a practical one.

Only the Fates could send me back to Earth, and all three of them had to be convinced if they were granting a request. Clotho spun the thread of a person's life, Lachesis measured it, and then Atropos cut the thread when somebody died and placed it on the tapestry of life. They were the only beings in the universe who could let you escape the Dream Realm. Even the gods were beholden to their will…

…but there was a limit to even the Fate's power.

They could not raise the dead, which was why I had to remain in Urgu after I visited them. Once you were dead on Earth, you could not return to the realm of the living.

Any other type of request was left to their discretion, and in the past hundred years since the disappearance of Hypnos, they had seen no travelers. Thus, K'dech was nearly abandoned. Hardly any of the shops survived, except for the Happy Dragon Inn. Some say it was enchanted to prevent hardship by Hypnos himself, because even in the depths of winter, the Happy Dragon was packed to the gills, as if people transported in and out of the Happy Dragon without visiting the rest of the town. Of course, that kind of magic was impossible for anyone but the Wicked Witch.

"Can I ask you a question?" Rose said as I pushed open the heavy, wooden door to the inn. "Do you have to sleep?"

"That is a silly question, and one that will likely get you discovered as a new traveler here. If any here find out who you are, the entire tavern will turn on us."

"Why?"

"Because many of them work as mercenaries or bounty hunters, and your capture will bring a pretty penny from the queen."

"Wonderful."

"They are not good people, but they are not bad, either. They are just trying to get by, however they can."

"Evening, Red!" A broad, thickly mustached orc called from behind the bar.

"Sam'il," I said, shaking his clawed hand. "How are you, my friend?"

"Busy, as always. Should I get you your usual?"

I nodded. "Two, please. And a quiet place to put my feet up if you wouldn't mind."

Sam'il's sharp, green fingers pointed to the corner, where three men were drinking beers on bearskin stools. "I'll get those guys to move."

"Appreciated."

By the time Sam'il gave me my two flagons, a barback had moved the drunken men along and we took their spot by the fire. I reached into my bag and pulled out a handful of glowing pink orbs. I started to count them, thought better of it, and handed all of them to Sam'il.

"Thank you, my friend, for your discretion."

Sam'il looked down at the orbs in his hand. "That buys a lot of discretion."

"Please remember that, should push come to shove," I said. Sam'il nodded and walked away.

I passed one of the flagons over to Rose. "Drink up."

She held up her hands. "I'm sorry. I'm not a beer kind of person."

"It's not beer."

"Then, what is it?"

I smiled. "It's whatever you want it to be."

She didn't believe me, and that was okay. She drank it anyway. "Oh my god. It tastes like lavender tea. How did you know I loved lavender tea?"

"It's a trick of your mind." I look a sip of my bitterroot beer then leaned in closer to Rose. "I didn't answer your question earlier, but I will now. You do not have to eat, drink, or sleep here, but your mind believes you do, and so it behooves you to indulge it. The less you act like a human, including partaking of the needs of humanity, the more painful it will become for you. However, I once stayed in the heights of the Lithdari mountains for six months without food, drink, or shelter, and I am still here. If your mind is sharp and your will strong, you can withstand nearly anything."

"Except death," Rose said, taking another sip.

I looked down at the flagon of beer in my hands. "There is tale that with the right mental strength, one can even prevent death itself. However, I have never met the man who could deny Thanatos when he comes to reap."

"Thanatos?"

"The god of Death, at least for my people. I believe the reason we evaporate here when we die is because Thanatos cannot come to bring us home, and without him, our souls just fade away."

"That is dark," Rose said, her eyes wide.

"I'm sorry."

"No," she replied with a smile. "I like dark. Have you met my girlfriend?"

I took another sip of my ale. "I can see why the gorgon likes you."

She chuckled. "That makes one of us. I just try to remember how lucky I am to have her."

Rose looked toward the door, as if hoping it would open and her beau would be on the other side. I turned to look, too, and for a moment, I got caught in her hope. I wanted the same for her.

The door did open, but unfortunately, it was not good news. Instead of Chelle, the green armor of the Nimue's guards stepped over the threshold. There were two of them, and likely more outside.

I spoke without moving. "Put your drink down carefully and stand up. Don't act suspicious."

"Bandits and ruffians," the fair-haired guard shouted from the door, "we are not looking for trouble. If we get what we want, we'll be on our way."

An ugly old gnome with only one good eye shouted into the bottom of his beer. "Piss off!"

The guard smirked, stomped oved to the gnome, and sliced him in half with one flick of the wrist. The gnome vanished into the ether, and the rest of the tavern stood and drew their weapons.

"I'm sure you think you're good with those weapons. I promise you I am better. I will slay you all where you stand without a second thought. Or you could give us what we want, and we will be on our way."

I pulled Rose down to the ground and inched her toward the bar. Sam'il hid a trap door near the bar for these kinds of escapes, and I hoped that he'd left it open. I paid him quite a bit of dreams to cover for me.

"What do you want?" Sam'il snarled from the other side of the bar. With his hidden hand, he beckoned me forward.

"Finally, a man of reason. Thank you, good sir. I look for one among you who was headed this way. She would be traveling with The Red Rider. I assume you know of whom I speak?"

"I do," he said as I lifted the trap door and slid Rose inside. "She was here but left some time ago. I don't remember where she went."

"I do!" one of the drunks we forced to move spat out from the other side of the bar. "She was right over there not five minutes ago."

By the time he pointed, I was through the trap door and had it latched tight behind me. I don't know how we would meet Chelle now, but I couldn't keep Rose at the Happy Dragon. We had to make it to Ozma. That was the only place the dreamer would be safe.

CHAPTER 35
CHELLE

I'd never seen a giant in real life until I sat on the top of the hill overlooking the campsite where Diedre's people were being kept prisoner. They were a lot bigger than I imagined. Uglier, too. Hair covered every part of their body, even their foreheads. They were like walking werewolves, but twenty feet high. Behind the giant were four cages packed so tightly with Diedre's men that they couldn't even sit.

"Are you ready for this?" Diedre asked me as we looked over the encampment.

"No." I shook my head. "I'd never taken out more than a couple monster hunters before I came to Urgu. I can't take on a giant."

"Hey," she said. "You took on a dragon and won."

"By dumb luck!" My eyes went wide. "Stupid luck, really."

"That's more than we've had before. Just think about what comes next. Finish this for me and then I'll have my men take you to that inn to meet your girlfriend."

"Nuh uh. You're taking me, personally, if we get out of this."

"Fine," she said with a sour expression. "I'll take you. Just remember, we're counting on you."

I looked behind her to see forty men and women ready for battle. They squeezed their weapons, staring at the giant with bloodlust. I bit my lip, trying to block the thoughts plaguing me. I was going to get them all killed.

"Just keep the giant busy while we rescue our men, okay?" Diedre said, pushing me forward.

"Now, go."

I leapt up and over the hill. Once I engaged the beast, the rest of them were going to come down and open the cages to let out their friends, or countrymen, or whatever they were to each other.

"*Sonum augue!*" I shouted as a fireball shot out of my hand and slammed into the giant's chest. The giant turned to me, confused. "*Sonum augue!*"

More fireballs shot out of my hands, but they didn't hurt the giant. They connected with him without causing any damage, like I was lobbing Nerf balls at him. He lumbered forward, and the ground quaked. Behind me, the men tumbled down the hill as if their feet had been taken out from under them.

"*Reformabit pulverem luto!*" I screamed, touching the ground. The ground cracked and twisted under me, until the grass under the giant's foot turned to mud. "*Reditus!*"

The ground under the giant spun again, and then it returned to its normal state, except the giant's foot was stuck underneath it.

"AHHH!" the giant shouted, trying to pick up its foot once… twice…the third time, his foot exploded out of the ground, sending me falling backwards while bits of dirt and debris shot everywhere. The giant slammed his foot on the ground. More rock flung through the air and hit two of Diedre's men, who fell to the ground.

"Do something!" Diedre said.

"*Tutela obice!*" I screamed. A bright blue light emanated from my hands and formed a protective barrier between me and the giant. The giant lifted its hand and crashed down on the barrier, which cracked, but didn't break.

"It's working!" Diedre shouted. "Hurry up!"

Even with a full day to rest, I only had so much stamina, and casting powerful spells was like running a marathon. I couldn't keep it up for much longer. It took everything I had to maintain the barrier. Panting from the exertion, I saw men and women scrambling up the hill, their cages now empty. They'd been saved.

"Come on," Diedre called to me.

I used what remained of my might to push the barrier toward the giant. He struggled to stay upright, but with one final nudge I pushed him to the ground, and he slammed down onto the earth with a mighty crash. With the giant down, I turned back to Diedre and climbed back up the hill to safety.

CHAPTER 36

NIMUE

Hera had been generous to me in the time since I began to serve her, but none of her gifts were as great as the magic mirror on my bedroom wall. With a simple command, I could look upon any of those in my employ. It would have been more convenient if I could simply look and find the impetuous girl, but my eyes could only see through those that granted me the ability to use their minds freely.

Hera once told me that free will was a gift from the gods, and thus even the gods could not break it. Only those who gave it up willingly could be molded to my will. Given the powers I was granted, it was hard to complain about something so trivial, but it was still a nuisance, and I hated nuisances.

Those who worked for me gave up free will when they joined my cabal. I couldn't have them questioning my commands, after all. That would be madness. I had been betrayed too many times over the centuries to simply trust them. No. It was much better to take their free will, so they blindly carried out my commands. That made sure things got done.

Well, it usually made sure that things got done. Every once in a while, things didn't go my way.

"Show me my forces at the Happy Dragon Inn," I snarled at the mirror, stalking toward it with all the confidence of the rightful queen of Oz. By now, the girl would be under my control. But when I saw the inn, I found that my men had failed again to capture her.

"Play backward and show me everything that happened since my men walked into the inn," I commanded. The mirror moved backward in time until the moment my men arrived. There, I saw her. In the corner. The Red Rider. The girl sat next to her. She was pretty, but nothing too ravishing. She seemed absolutely and incredibly normal.

"How could they have gotten away?" I fumed. "They're right there! Continue from here, mirror. Do not change this angle."

The mirror replayed the scene. I watched as they slaughtered a drunken gnome, and then I watched the Red Rider take the girl through a small hatch at the base of the floor. My eyes narrowed.

"Move backwards again. This time, show me the barkeep."

The mirror played backwards and tilted to the north. When the image played again, I watched the barkeep turn slightly toward the Red Rider. I watched again, and this time I saw him beckon her forward. They were in this together. He helped the Red Rider and the girl escape.

"Guard!" Two burly oafs rushed inside. "Make contact with Captain Balsim. Burn the Happy Dragon to the ground. Tell him to bring the orc to me."

"Yes, ma'am."

"I will be there momentarily to examine the wreckage."

The guards left and I turned back to the mirror. I couldn't wait to watch the Happy Dragon go up in flames. It was a favorite place of Hypnos, and nothing brought me more pleasure than watching what he built turned to cinder.

CHAPTER 37

ROSE

"We can't just leave," I pleaded with Red. We were crouched behind a line of horses across from the Happy Dragon Inn, peeking through to see what was happening.

"We can't stay here, either."

"If we leave without her, then she'll get arrested—or worse!"

Red turned to me. "And what would you have me do? You are my charge, she is not. Had she not chosen to leave and defend those fighters, we would still be together."

"She left to save those people. You told me we were all in this together!"

Red curled her lip. "Those people were already dead. They were dead the moment they ended up here. This is nothing but a waystation for the damned, and we are just biding our time until we can join eternity."

"If you believe that, then why haven't you killed yourself yet, huh? You said you've been in Urgu over a thousand years, and yet, you're still here."

Red didn't have an answer and I knew it. To be honest, I wasn't interested even if she had a perfect response. She needed to figure out how we were going to tell Chelle where we were and what we were doing. I couldn't just leave her to be found and captured by the Wicked Witch.

"I will send somebody back for her," Red said. "Once we meet Ozma."

"And what if they capture her before then?"

"Damn it," Red said, giving my arm a menacing squeeze. "I am trying to be polite. Please believe me when I say that your girlfriend, while brave, is dead. Nobody can take on a full-grown dragon and live to tell about it. Not by themselves, anyway."

I yanked my arm free of her grasp. "You don't know Chelle."

"No, but I've seen enough foolhardy adventurers to know a dead one when I see one."

"If that's true, I might as well just kill myself." I stood up and bolted across the street. Before I reached the other side, Red tackled me and rolled me into the shelter of a house.

"You're going to get yourself killed," she hissed.

"I know! You don't understand. Without Chelle, none of this is worth anything. If she's dead, then I would rather die, too."

It was the truth but saying it out loud caused knots to form in my stomach. My body convulsed from the thought of losing the love of my life. I expected some sort of sympathy from Red, but instead she just started laughing.

"Stop laughing at me," I said, tears falling down my face.

Her laughter became a light chuckle. "You really are a spoiled brat, aren't you?"

"Excuse me? You have no idea what I've been through."

Red shrugged. "You're right, I don't. But whatever happened turned you into a spoiled brat. Do you not even understand what we're trying to do here? We're trying to stop the Wicked Witch from ending the universe as we know it. Do you really think your stupid crush is more important than that?"

"No. Love is more important than anything. Without Chelle, I'd rather just die," I said, wiping my face with the back of my hand.

"Besides, if I'm dead, I'm not your problem anymore. It's a win-win."

Red glared at me a few moments before speaking. "Idiot. You have a role to play in all of this. I don't know what it is yet, but you didn't come here for just no reason. Nobody does."

"Then why did you come here?"

Her lip twitched, like she wanted to say something, but then from across the street she saw the Queen's Guard pulling Sam'il out of the bar. He had been beaten and could barely walk. The head guard tossed him into the street.

"Now you'll watch," the guard said, "as your precious bar and everybody inside turns to dust."

"Hypnos will never allow you to do that. His power protects us here!"

The guard punched Sam'il across the face. "He's been dead for a hundred years. It doesn't matter if he cares, because he's nothing but dust."

"He's not dead! He will return, and there will be a reckoning for all who oppose him!"

The guard snapped his fingers and I heard a familiar screech from the sky. My heart sank. The leather wings of a dragon descended upon us and perched on the house right above where we were hiding.

"Burn it down!" the guard shouted.

With one breath, the dragon torched the Happy Dragon. Thirty seconds of fire later, the entire bar was in flames, and the people inside screamed in agony as they burned alive.

The guard watched, a nasty smirk on his face. He turned to Sam'il, who was staring in horror. "Where is your precious god now?" It was clear that Hypnos was nowhere to be found.

"At least they left Chelle a clear sign," Red said. "When she sees this, she'll know something was wrong."

I looked over at Red. "And you'll send somebody back for her?"

She nodded. "On my honor."

"There doesn't seem to be much of that these days."

"That, my friend, is what we are trying to fix."

As we disappeared into the night, the screams from the Happy Dragon died out. Every life inside was wiped from Urgu, and from the universe.

CHAPTER 38
CHELLE

I didn't know how to ride a horse well, but that didn't matter much, as the only other way to find Rose was walking, which I found even more distasteful.

The nice thing about riding a horse in the Dream Realm was that no matter how long I rode, I didn't get stiff or sore. I had only ridden a horse once before, and even after ten minutes my thighs were aching. Diedre and I had been on horseback for over two hours and I didn't need to rest or recover. That part was nice. One point for Urgu, a thousand points against it.

"So," Diedre said, riding next to me, "am I to believe that the red rider with you was an agent of Ozma?"

"I think so," I said, uncertain. "Honestly, things have been happening so quickly it's hard to know what to believe."

Diedre clenched the reigns of her saddle. "I wish I had known that. I would have killed her myself."

"You don't like Ozma?"

Diedre shook her head vehemently. "I don't like royalty, or rulers at all. I've fought battles in my day, and had enough people fight for me, that I know these rulers are more trouble then they're worth."

"Better than the Wicked Witch, though, right?"

Diedre sneered. "That's like saying poison is better than beheading. They are both part of the same broken system. Honestly, on some level I prefer my rulers outwardly evil. At least then they don't hide it."

"I don't much like kings either," I replied. "We don't have that in America."

Diedre chuckled. "Ah, yes. You have democracy still. That's what it's called, right?"

"That's right."

Diedre grinned. "I have met my share of Americans over the last two hundred years. You truly are the most gullible people in the world."

I glared at her. "Gullible? I am not gullible."

Diedre threw her head back and laughed. "Sure you are, Chelle. You believe you are free, even though you are ruled in much the same way we are ruled. It's just under the guise of freedom, so your kings can more easily maintain control."

I snickered. "Dude, I'm a nihilist, but that's dark even for me."

She shrugged. "I hope I am wrong, though I am not."

"What would you do, then? If you were in charge?"

"I wouldn't be in charge. That's the point."

I rolled my eyes. "You seem in charge to me. You had all those people fight for you back when we fought that giant and saved your people from those cages. They risked their lives for you."

"I happen to be a leader, but I am not in charge. If I were in charge, though, I would burn it all down."

"Anarchy, then?"

Diedre paused to consider for a moment. "I quite like that word. What does it mean?"

"It's mayhem."

A smile crested on Diedre's face. "Yes, I very much like that. If I were to burn it all down, only mayhem would remain."

I chuckled. "There are plenty of movies about that. It usually ends up not very good for the characters in them."

Diedre cocked her head. "What's a movie?"

"It's like a book with moving pictures."

Diedre scratched her head. "Hrm, like a play, then?"

"Sure, kinda."

"Then the principle is the same." Diedre chuckled. "Who do you think funds those stories? The people that control the system. That's what I'm trying to tell you. Same thing with books and songs and everything else ever created. Even the stories you heard—fairy tales, I think you call them—were manipulated by rulers to keep their sheep docile. For instance, do you know the tale of *Beauty and the Beast?*"

"Of course," I replied with a slight bit of disgust. "Everybody does. You don't know what this is, but there was a Disney movie about it. Two, in fact. The animated one was better."

Diedre stared at me blankly. "I barely understand any of the words that you just said, but I'll assume that's a yes."

I nodded slowly. "That's a yes."

Diedre pulled the reins of her horse until it stopped in front of me. "Did you know that story was created in order to teach children that arranged marriages were good. The beast represented the rich husband which could be tamed with love and become a prince. That story was mind control, and it seems to have worked, even into your animated movies."

"That's crazy."

Diedre nodded before flicking the reins so that her horse would move again. "That is the power of the ruling class. They can keep a story going forever as long as it serves their purpose. I never wanted that life. I told my father—I begged him to let me marry outside of nobility—I saw how it corrupted."

"You were a ruler?"

Diedre's eyes dropped to the ground. "The daughter of one, but I gave it up to be with the man I loved. My betrothed was so angry at my slight of him that he started a war to win me back. He could have had any woman in the kingdom, but I was the fairest, and I defied him—so he needed me. Of course, none of that mattered in the end. I didn't matter in the end. I was just property, like a prized cow."

I couldn't believe it. "That's horrible."

Deidre shrugged. "I knew what I was getting into when I ran off. It was worth it for one day of freedom. I still love that man with every bone in my body."

"That's how I feel about Rose."

Diedre nodded. "Then we have to win her back for you. Good news, the Happy Dragon is right—"

But she didn't finish her sentence. Instead, her jaw went slack. In front of us both was the horrible ruins of the Happy Dragon, charred and burnt to rubble. A dragon sat on the roof of a house across the street from it, happily chomping on the remains of a goat.

"Rose!" I screamed, but Diedre reached over and muffled my words.

"Don't say another word. We'll figure out what happened, but you have to act calm, even though there is a fire raging inside of you."

I didn't know if I could act cool, but I would try. My bones told me that Rose wasn't dead. The odds were bleak, but I knew she wasn't dead.

CHAPTER 39
RED

Bang. Bang. Bang.

It had taken us the rest of the night to get to Balor's hut. He was the closest friendly agent of Ozma, the rightful heir, at least the closest one still alive. I hoped he was still alive. I hadn't seen my old friend in over a decade, but he always had a warm grog of mead and a roaring fire whenever I needed him.

"Quit yer yappin'!" Balor shouted from the other side of the door. When the handle turned, there was my friend, built like an ox with a long, bushy, red beard. "Evening, Belle. What do you want?"

"That any way to speak to an old friend?"

He shook his head. "Probably not, but we can't be much of friends since I haven't seen ya in a decade."

"I'm sorry. That lapse is on me. I have been busy in the hinterlands and mountains for Ozma."

Balor's face cracked, and he smiled. "I'm just kiddin', ya ole so and so. C'mere." He wrapped me in a hug so tight I worried my ribs might crack.

"Too tight."

Balor dropped me, and his eyes fixed on Rose. "And who is this lovely lass?"

I squared my shoulders. "I'm afraid I need something from you. This girl...she came through the barrier between Earth and Urgu."

"My god," Balor replied, shocked. "There hasn't been one since—"

"A hundred years. To the day. Nearly the minute when he went missing. Just like the prophesy foretold."

"So, it is true, then. The prophesy."

"It looks that way." I looked back at Rose. "Of course, it could just be a coincidence."

"Ain't no coincidences, lass. You know that."

"Excuse me," Rose said. "Can somebody tell me what's going on?"

Balor gave me an inquisitive look, then his eyes turned to her. "You better come in. These are dangerous times and I'd rather not say anything where there are prying eyes and ears."

Balor moved away from the door to let us inside. His home was just as I remembered, with the same bear skin rug and poorly constructed wooden table. The fire raged so hot that I had to take off my cloak and place it on the hanger next to the door before I even sat down. Of course, that was Balor's intention. He was of the fire, so the heat never bothered him, so if somebody came into his home, they would be at a disadvantage immediately.

"Sit," Balor said, gesturing to the chairs scattered around his table. "I will bring the mead, and we will toast to the end of these times."

"I'm not sure we should be toasting yet," I replied, but he was already pouring the flagons.

"Maybe you're right." He brought one over and handed it to me. "Then we should drink to forget these miserable times."

"Can somebody please explain to me what's going on?" Rose said. "What is this about a prophesy?"

Balor brought another flagon for Rose and then sat down with his own. "I assume you know about Hypnos."

"That he disappeared," Rose said, placing down her mead. "Yes."

"And how Hera took over."

"I told her, friend," I said.

"Then I can skip ahead," Balor wiped the foam off his beard. "Good. I hate tellin' stories."

"Liar." I laughed. I had listened to him tell stories about his conquests for hours as we sat in front of the roaring fire. I barely said a word as he waxed on about his life.

"Many thought he died, perhaps by the hand of Hera herself. However, some of us, like me, knew that you could never kill a god. Not really. They are energy. They created life itself, and Hypnos was especially strong here, as this was his domain. For years we searched for him, and then, one day, the Fates intervened."

"I thought they never opened their tower."

"They did, only once, twenty years ago, to relay a message to me. They told me that one hundred years after the disappearance of Hypnos, a dreamer would come who would bring him back again."

"That's all they said?" Rose asked in a huff.

"There were more specifics, but that was the gist. That is why you are so important." I turned to her. "I think you might be able to bring back Hypnos and save the world."

Rose shook her head. "That's stupid. I can barely tie my shoes, let alone save the world. I don't even know this world. How can I save it?"

I shrugged. "We don't know. That's why I must take you to Ozma, she will know how we should proceed. After all, the Fates themselves bestowed the prophesy upon her. The rest of us only got the information second hand."

"I will go with you," Rose said after a long pause. "I already told you I would. But not without Chelle."

"We can't wait for her," I said, forcefully. "If she is alive, of which there is a very small hope, then she will be days behind us."

"I don't care."

"What is a Chelle?" Balor said after a long sip of ale.

"She's Rose's girlfriend. She came through the gates of Urgu from Earth to find Rose and bring her to the Obsidian Spindle."

"Wow," Balor said, clearly impressed. "That's some woman."

"And...she has magic."

Balor slammed his beer down on the table. "No. She doesn't."

I nodded, my eyes wide with excitement. "She might be powerful enough to rival the queen herself."

"Ha! That's incredible. Maybe we'll stand a chance yet."

"Will you go and find her?" I asked. "She's at the Happy Dragon Inn. Or what is left of it. It's been burned down."

Balor choked in disbelief. "Burned down?"

I nodded slowly. "By a dragon, no less."

Balor smirked. "Poetic justice, I'll give it that. Took a dragon to destroy a dragon. Even Hypnos would have appreciated the irony."

"It shows that Hypnos's power had faded." I leaned in toward Balor. "I need a favor from you."

"I would expect nothing else."

"Will you go find out if Chelle is alive? And if she is, bring her to the sanctuary?"

Balor nodded. "Aye."

I turned to Rose. "Is that enough to get you to come with me? He knows where to meet us. He knows everything I know, and much more."

"I'm still not sure if I should trust you," Rose said after a moment.

"That's a good instinct, lass," Balor said. "You shouldn't trust anybody, but we are a more trustful lot than most. Certainly, more so than the queen. More important, we can get you to the Obsidian Spindle. Nobody else can do that."

"If you do that, then I will go with you," Rose said. "But I'm not helping you until I see Chelle."

"And what if she be dead?" Balor asked. "What then?"

"She's alive. I know it."

"Then I will find her and bring her to you. Of that I swear."

"If you swear it," Rose said to Balor before turning to me, "then I suppose I will trust you."

"You have no other option."

"Sure I do. I could refuse."

Balor laughed. "I doubt Red would let you do that."

This time, it was Rose who laughed. "She hasn't known me very long. I can be very stubborn."

"Then it's a good thing I agreed," I said.

Balor nodded. "That it is."

"If this is settled, then we all must hurry." I got to my feet. "There is no time to lose. Hopefully the next time we see each other, the Fates will have smiled on us."

Balor tilted his head back and finished his ale. "To that day," he said, shaking my hand. "To that day."

CHAPTER 40

CHELLE

After we dismounted, we tied the horses near the tree line. We didn't want them to be food for a hungry dragon, after all. Once they were safe, we made our way back to the burned ruin of the Happy Dragon.

"That building stood for over a thousand years," Diedre said. "We thought it was invincible."

"Then what happened to it?"

"Hypnos's magic weakens every day. His will protected this place, and now that will has faded to nothing." A smirk broadened across her face. "Maybe he truly is dead."

It didn't matter why the place burned down. What mattered was that Rose could have been inside, and I had to find out if she was dead or not.

"We need to get a closer look."

"Why?"

"To see if Rose…"

"She won't be here. Even if she's dead, it's not like her body is going to show up. If she's dead, she's ash. If she's alive, she's either gone from this place or captured."

Captured. I didn't think about captured, but it only made sense that they would have taken prisoners before they burned the inn to the ground.

"Where would they keep their prisoners?" I asked.

"Behind about fifty guards, locked in a prison carriage."

I looked around the town for any sign of a prison carriage, but I couldn't find any. "I'm going in. Wait here."

"Are you kidding?" Deidre said. "You're about as stealthy as a two-ton bison. You'll be caught in a second, and then they'll look around for me. We need help."

"I need to find Rose."

The dragon high above was resting comfortably, the carcass of a freshly eaten goat lay on the ground in front of it. I crept into the town and ducked into a little nook on the side of thatch-roofed house. I listened for guards but couldn't make out anything.

When I'd reached the other side of the house, I peered around the corner. Two guards were trying desperately not to fall asleep and failing. Finally, they were both leaning against the house, dozing. I leapt from one building to the other.

The charred remains of the Happy Dragon lay in front of me. I heard voices from the other side of the building.

"Have you found them yet?"

A woman's voice answered. "No, sir."

I peeked around the corner and saw a tall, blonde man. His emerald breast plate was embossed with a golden peacock. He was talking to a shorter woman in leather armor with a similar emblem on her chest.

"Keep looking."

"We've looked over every inch of this city and...nothing. Maybe she burned up or dusted."

"Then find her ashes!" the man shouted in her face.

"Yes, sir," the woman replied, visibly shaken.

The man turned away. There was a crack in the air followed by a flash, and suddenly, in front of the man was the Wicked Witch. She was dressed in a long black gown and wearing a headdress of hooked horns.

"I am displeased," the witch said.

"Queen Nimue," the man said, genuflecting. "It is an honor."

"Get up!" Nimue said. "You can't find the girl on your knees." Nimue held out her arm, and the man slowly rose to his feet as if not by his own power. The witch was levitating him. "Of course, you can't find her without your head, either."

The man's face turned purple. "Yes, queen."

Nimue flicked her wrists and the man fell, gasping for air. "You have never disappointed me before, Captain Balsim. I assume that is because you know the way I deal with incompetence."

Captain Balsim stayed on the ground, holding his neck and panting. "I do, ma'am. I live only to serve you."

"Good..." Nimue trailed off. She lifted her nose into the air and sniffed. "I smell something. Something—oh, this is delicious."

Something tugged on my shirt. I turned around to find Diedre. "Come on. We have to go. Nimue—"

"I know she's here," I said, pointing to her on the other side of the charred rubble. "I can see her."

Diedre peeked around the corner. "We gotta move."

"I think you're right."

I turned to move, but I was stuck in place. Something dragged me backwards against my will. Nimue was holding her hands in the air, beckoning me forward with her fingers. Next to me, Diedre grunted and kicked her invisible restraints.

"My, my, my. Don't you get around," Nimue said.

I lifted my arms to cast a spell, but Nimue clasped her hands tightly and my arms snapped close to my body, unable to move.

"I never thought I would see you again." Nimue looked me up and down and then her eyes settled on the amulet around my neck. "I smell old magic on you, girl. Why do you hide your true form?"

"No, please," I said.

But she didn't listen. She took my amulet and crushed it with her free hand, keeping me and Diedre suspended in air with the other. With the amulet gone, I returned to my original form. My snakes curled through the air and hissed at Nimue.

"That's better," Nimue said, her voice pinched with excitement. "You are so much more beautiful in your true form. Tell me, does your friend know?"

I looked back at the shocked expression on Diedre's face. It was twisted into a fury. "You're a monster!" She spat. "How could you? I never would have—"

"Please," I said. "I'm only a half-monster. I'm not so—"

"Shut it!" Diedre said. "If we get outta here, I'm gonna cut off your head myself."

"Well," Nimue said, chuckling. "I would very much like to see that, but I think she has more use to me than just as a trophy. Don't you?" Nimue took another deep whiff in. "You have something else that I haven't seen in even longer...you have a body."

Diedre gasped. "A body? You were stupid enough to come to Urgu of your own free will? You really are stupid."

I nodded. "Seems that way."

Nimue smiled. "Do you know that I've been searching for a body for over a thousand years. There is one particular spell that I've been meaning to try. It could be the answer to everything. Balsim!"

Captain Balsim ran forward. "Yes, my lady."

"Bring this one to my castle. Take her friend, too. They could both be of use to me yet. Besides, if my spell doesn't work, I would very much like to see the red-haired one cut off the gorgon's head."

CHAPTER 41
NIMUE

After capturing the magic user and her friend, I travelled back to my library. There was no hurry to summon the prisoners. They could rot in my dungeon.

In the meantime, I needed to find the right spell in all my notes. It had not been part of my plan, but when I realized the girl had a physical body, my mind crackled alive with the possibilities.

Hera had given me unlimited power to help her break out of the Dream Realm and return to the universe, but I still did not have enough power to succeed, which meant I needed to find another way. I didn't necessarily want an angry god roaming the universe, and I just wanted to return to Earth in any way I could. If that meant working with Hera, then so be it, but there were other ways to return to Earth and I had studied them all. I only helped her because there was no other option.

I walked to the back of the room and flicked through a stack of old books until I found the one I was looking for. Wiping the dust and soot from the book, I cracked it open and started skimming. I had made meticulous notes on every page, but carefully—the book was older than almost anything in the library. Older than me. For all I knew, it was older than Hera as well.

I found the passage I needed. *Soul binding: A method of necromancy which binds a soul into a living host body, effectively extracting the original soul and allowing the new one to manipulate the body.*

The gorgon girl had a body and a soul, which meant she also had the spark of the gods, and that made her the most powerful being in all Urgu, save for the gods themselves. With her power combined with me, even the Fates could not keep the door to their keep closed from me.

CHAPTER 42
ROSE

Red and I walked through the night until we came upon an odd church. It slanted to the right at an acute angle and the tip of its steeple, curled like the tail of a pig, seemed to point to the top of the tallest peak of the mountain range in the distance. The building was painted six different colors: red, blue, green, purple, yellow, orange, and it continued in that order up the entire base and into the sky.

"That is a weird structure," I said when it became clear we were walking toward it.

"It's the Church of the Six," Red said. "They worship the six deities of Urgu."

"Hedging their bets."

"In a way. However, unlike Earth, these gods actually presented themselves and visited their wrath upon the people quite often, so appeasing them is not the worst idea in the world."

"Do you worship the six gods?" I asked as we neared the entrance. It was a wooden door with six faces carved on it.

"I do not worship any god." Red sneered. "They are fickle and cruel."

"Is this them?" I asked, pointing to the door.

Red nodded. She indicated a thin-faced man with smoke coming out of his head. "That is Hypnos, the abandoner." Next to him was a woman, scowling. "Hera the cruel." Below her was the picture of a lioness. "Sekmet the hunter." Next to the lion was a wide faced man with spider legs growing out of his head. "Anansi the sly." Below Anansi was an androgynous man with horns growing out of his head. "Loki the Trickster." And finally a woman with blood on her face. "And Agrona the Merciless. The six gods of Urgu, each worse than the last. Come now. We are late."

Red pushed open the door and walked inside. Wooden pews made up the majority of the inside decor, besides an altar at the far end with six bowls beneath it. Painted reliefs adorned every wall, depicting the gods engaged in battle. A nude Agrona stood covered in blood, holding the head of a deer. Anansi hung as a spider from a tree, whispering to a child. Loki sat on a throne of glass. Hera held the world in her hands. Sitting at the top of the church, watching the others like a guardian, was Hypnos.

Red walked to the altar with its six golden bowls on the ground. She pulled out six pink orbs from her pouch and held them up.

"What are those?" I asked.

"They are dreams, the currency of Urgu."

"Dreams? Like...my dreams...like when I stand in front of the class without pants on and people laugh at me kind of dreams?"

Red chuckled. "Those are nightmares. That is Epiales's domain. These are dreams. The kind that leave you untethered to the world and in a blissful state of peace. That is the true nature of Urgu, not this bastardization it has become."

"I watched you hand some of those to the orc at the Happy Dragon Inn. Do you barter with them, too?"

Red threw a dream into each of the altars. "They are very power-ful, Rose. Dreams hold every secret in the universe. They are truth and they are falsehood. There is nothing greater in all of Urgu aside from the Obsidian Spindle, so yes, we barter with them. Now that there are no more dreams coming to Urgu, their value increases by the day."

Red bent down and placed her hand in each altar. I heard a cracking and saw a mist of pink ascend as she broke one dream off in each bowl.

"You destroy them?"

"They are power. If you want to summon something powerful, you must use power itself. We trade them until an opportunity comes to use them."

"That is an odd currency."

"Perhaps, but is it so different from your dollar? It is a piece of paper that you think represents value, but it is not but what you imagine it to be. These dreams, however, have real power."

I sucked in my breath and held it for a moment, studying the church and all of its paintings and bowls and altars. "This place is so weird."

Red let out a breathy laugh. "You haven't seen anything yet."

The six wisps of dreams found each other in the middle of the temple. They molded together into a thin tendril which rose high into the air, disappearing into the bent steeple.

Red sat down in one of the pews, cupping her hands together like she was praying. She closed her eyes and muttered something that I couldn't understand. Then, she placed her head in her hands and took a deep breath.

"What do we do now?" I asked.

"We wait."

CHAPTER 43

CHELLE

"I'm sorry I lied to you." I muttered to Diedre from the back of the prison carriage. She was tied to the front of the carriage, a few feet away. We had been riding for hours and the bumps in the ground were making me nauseous.

"Don't talk to me, monster."

"I don't like how you are saying that word. I'm not a monster, at least not in that way. I mean, I am technically a monster, but we're not all bad."

Diedre turned toward the front of the coach where there was a small window with thick bars on it. I could see the driver of the carriage through it, and the two horses. "That's not been my experience. Every time I've come up against a monster, they have attacked me. Like that dragon!"

"Yeah? And you attacked first! I've never hunted a human. They're the ones who hunt me."

"No, no! You were there on the road. You saw it—that dragon came out of nowhere."

"*After* you attacked the dream changer's carriage. And yes, I was there. I saved your life. Do you remember that?"

"I never should have helped you," she growled.

"You helped me because I helped you. If I hadn't, you would have been burned alive. And if I didn't help you with the giant, you'd have been ground to dust—you and all your friends. The least you could do is help me."

"And get captured in the process."

"It's better than being dead!"

"Is it?" Diedre asked, leaning toward me and speaking in a strained whisper. "Do you have any idea what the queen will do to us when she gets us back to her castle?"

"I have some idea. I saw what they did to Rose before we rescued her."

"It's going to be horrible."

"So is this conversation," I grumbled.

Diedre leaned back against the carriage. "This is why I hate rulers. They think they can just kill their people and it's not going to matter. They think we don't matter."

"I get it. You hate kings. If we get out of here then you can complain all you want, but first, let's get out of here."

Diedre slumped in her seat. "How? The queen enchanted this carriage herself so you can't use magic."

I shrugged. "It hasn't stopped me before. I used magic when I was with the pixies."

Diedre scoffed at me. "Pixies are arrogant and vain. Two things the Wicked Witch is not."

"I met her," I growled at her. "She's both of those things."

"She's also smart."

I cocked my head to the right. "So, you're what? Just going to lay back and accept your death?"

Diedre turned away from me. "I laid back and accepted it before. That's how I ended up here. I don't see why I can't do it again."

I chuckled. "If only it worked. Then I wouldn't have to be hearing this stupid conversation."

"Just shut up and leave me alone."

I leaned in toward her. "I would love to, but you're the only one here, and I need your help if I'm going to escape."

Diedre gave me a cold look. "You're not going to escape."

I crossed my arms. "Says you. I've escaped worse than this."

"You are cocky," Diedre said, shaking her head. "I'll give you that."

"Thank you."

"That wasn't a compliment. I hate cocky. Cocky gets people killed."

I was done talking with her. I would just get out of the handcuffs by myself. Then, I would get out of this carriage and leave her to rot with the queen. I yanked on the chains, just as I had a dozen times before, but there was still no give in them.

Diedre pushed back against the wall of the carriage. "You're not just cocky, you're stupid, too. It's not going to work, Gorgon."

I looked up at her. The snakes on my head hissed at her, and the venom which dripped off her words. "I *am* a gorgon. Congratulations, you've correctly identified me, or at least half of me. The other half is human."

Diedre snarled at me. "I can't see that half. Just a disgusting monster."

I shook my head, sad but not surprised. "You humans are all the same. You hate what you don't understand."

The horses pulling our carriage whinnied and bucked. The carriage shook and I fell onto the ground of the carriage as it tilted from one side to the other.

"What's going on up there?" I asked.

Deidre pushed herself up and looked out the window. "I don't know. I can't really see much of anything."

Something slammed onto the hood of the carriage. The sides of the carriage crumpled as if it were a tube of toothpaste someone was squeezing.

"Hang on!"

The carriage lifted off the ground as I tumbled back and forth, its roof crunching down closer toward us. If we didn't get out soon, we would be killed for sure.

"Get back here!" I shouted to Diedre. The front of the carriage was nearly flattened, but I had some room in the back of the coach.

Diedre slid toward me just as the back door popped open like a can of Pringles. The carriage tilted and I slid down toward the opening until I hung out of the back of the cart. I heard a loud thud and looked up to see one of my snakes crying. It was Albert. One of his teeth was missing and the blood from his mouth dripped onto my head.

"Albie!" I wanted to help him, but I couldn't do anything while I was hanging on for dear life. The only thing that kept me from falling to the ground were the shackles that bound my hands.

"Ahh!" Diedre shouted as she tumbled out after me and latched onto my leg.

I looked up to see a Cyclops, orange and hairy, holding the carriage high into the air. My feet dangled, trying to find a foothold, but found nothing except sky. We were at least twenty feet off the ground. A fall of that height would probably kill me, but a Cyclops definitely would if we didn't break free and escape.

"I'm going to get us out of here." I grabbed onto the shackles and pulled myself up toward the cabin. "*Rubigo!*"

The shackles turned to rust in my hands, and I yanked myself free, leaving the manacles to shatter. I was free. I reached out my hand and grabbed onto Diedre's chain. I held onto her so that she wouldn't fall away when the metal rusted through.

"*Rubigo!*"

"Great, we're free," Diedre said, rubbing her wrists. "Now what?"

"You're not going to like this part."

"I haven't liked any of this!"

"Jump!"

I let go and plummeted to the ground, sure I was going to die. But the ground didn't break my fall. Instead of landing on the dirt, I dropped into the meaty palm of the Cyclops. Diedre fell next to me on its hand.

"Great," I said, standing up and ready to fight. "Now we're going to die."

"Are you Chelle?" the giant said.

I cocked my head. "That's me."

"Perfect," the Cyclops said. "Somebody is looking for you." He placed me on the ground, and I rolled onto to my feet. As I looked up, he shrunk into a normal sized man with a big, bushy red beard. He now had two eyes where he used to have one.

"Sorry for the theatrics. We don't have time for a proper rescue."

"Who are you?"

"Name's Balor. I'm a friend of Rose."

"Rose!" I said. "Where is she?"

"Come on," Balor said. "I'll take you to her." Balor looked over at Diedre. "Is she a friend of yours?"

I shook my head. "Not even a little, but we shouldn't leave her out here to die."

Balor shrugged. "Your call. I'd personally leave her for dead."

I held my hand out to help Diedre. "Come with me."

"I don't think so," Diedre said, ignoring my extended hand and getting to her feet on her own. "My place is with my people. I must return to them."

"You haven't really fulfilled your oath to help me. We haven't found Rose."

"That oath was broken the minute we were captured. As far as I'm concerned, we're square. This...gentleman—"

"—Balor."

"Balor can lead you the rest of the way."

"It's not safe out there."

"It's not safe anywhere. Haven't you learned anything?" She looked at me and twisted up her face. "And...thank you. For your help. Maybe you're right. Maybe all monsters aren't evil. Just most of them."

"I guess that's the best I'm going to get."

"Aye," Diedre said. "It's probably better than you deserve."

And with that she ran off, and I was left with a weird man who could turn into a cyclops. But he could also lead me back to Rose.

CHAPTER 44

RED

She has to come. She has to come. She has to come. Please come.

"What are you doing?" Rose asked, sliding into the pew next to me.

"Nothing."

"Oh. It just looked like you're praying, is all."

I sighed and looked up at the ceiling. "That is what I'm doing, Rose. I'm praying for aid."

"Why?"

I couldn't tell her that I had lied to her this whole time. I couldn't let her know that the great and powerful Ozma didn't believe in the prophesy when I told it to her, and she hadn't sent me to fetch Rose.

Ozma would believe me if I could give her proof, I knew it. And I had proof. The girl had come to Urgu a hundred years to the hour that the prophesy said she would. That wasn't a coincidence.

"I'm praying that Ozma hears my calls to her and sends me a sign of where to find her."

"What do you mean, find her?" I said, pissed off and confused. "I thought you knew where she was."

"I do," I lied. "However, she moves around so much to avoid the

Wicked Witch that we often need guidance to find which base she is hiding in.”

“That sounds stupid. Are you lying to me?”

I needed to keep the lie floating for a little while longer. Ozma would see the truth about the prophesy and I would be vindicated. She’d even apologize for thinking I was crazy. I would be the one who brought peace to Urgu again.

“I don’t think I’m capable of lying,” I said, lying again.

“Well that’s just not true. Everybody can lie. It’s only a matter of whether they’re good at it.”

“Fair enough. I have never been very good at lying.”

“I’ll bet you’re good at a lot of things with a thousand years to practice. Besides, if you were good at lying, you wouldn’t tell me. You would lie about it. Now, what’s really going on?”

Before I could answer the door opened. Ozma. Please let it be Ozma.

I turned around to look at who was coming inside, but when the door closed, it wasn’t Ozma standing before me. It was a half-gorgon with snakes for hair.

“Chelle!” Rose said, rushing up and wrapping her arms around the gorgon.

“Welcome back, Chelle,” I said. “You look like you have more snakes than last time I saw you.”

Chelle kissed Rose long and hard, then turned to me. “Nope. The same amount. What are you doing?”

“She’s trying to find Ozma,” Rose replied before I had a chance to do so.

“Wait,” Chelle said, her lip curling indignantly. “This whole time you’ve been leading us to her, and you don’t know where she is?”

A flash of light exploded through the church and I covered my eyes. When I looked again, the ceiling of the church was glistening with a thousand lights, like stars in the sky. They lit up the entire ceiling, each pinpoint light slowly fading until only one remained, emanating from the painting of Hypnos, directly on his forehead.

"That looks like a sign," Chelle said.

"It is," I replied, disappointed. "She's in the one place no sane person wants to go."

"Where is that?"

"Underneath Oz. Her first hiding spot after the usurper took her throne." Hopefully it would not be her last.

CHAPTER 45
NIMUE

"Don't look so sad, my pet," I said to Diedre. My men found her in the Mistreach and brought her to me. She took out a half-dozen of my men before they subdued her.

"I am not sad for me. My body is nothing. I am sad for my people."

"Yes, your people. Don't worry. They will be safe, as long as you do what I ask."

Diedre swallowed loudly. I could smell the fear coming off of her, but she was too proud to show it. "And what is that?"

I walked toward her slowly and deliberately. "Tell me where the girl is, that gorgon you were travelling with."

Diedre spun her head, avoiding eye contact. "I don't know..." she said with hurried breath. "There was a Cyclops, and the carriage crumpled...and then the monster left without me."

"That is sad." I stopped when I was in front of her and leaned down to whisper, "Perhaps I do need to pay closer attention to your people."

"No! Please," Diedre replied, tears forming in her eyes, "they have done nothing to you."

I scoffed. "They have been a scourge on me for years. It's best that I cut off the head and then drown the snake. Though, if you give me another snake, then perhaps they can live free for a while longer."

"We are just trying to survive." Diedre gritted her teeth. "Since the dreamers left, we were kicked out of our home. Please, we only want to live in peace."

"And yet you vandalize everything you come across." My voice boomed through the hall. "You are a bad subject of the crown, I must say. Yes, you will be made an example of. All of you."

"Please." Diedre cleared her throat. "What can I do to prove I am loyal, my queen?"

"Bring me the girl." I took my time with every word and let them each land on her pale cheek.

She took a long moment to respond. "I can't do that. I don't know where she is."

I sneered at her. "Then I will watch you and all you love burn to the ground."

Diedre held up her arms. "No! Wait. I may not have the girl, but I have something."

"What could you possibly have that will help me? Without the gorgon you are nothing."

Diedre pulled a long tooth out of her pocket. "One of her snakes lost this in the fight. You can use it to find her and end Ozma forever. Kill two birds with one stone. That's what you want, right?"

With the bones of the snake, I could create a pathway between the mirror and the girl. I could spy on her without the gorgon ever knowing and take my revenge on Ozma before escaping Urgu forever.

I snickered. "It's one of the things I need." I held up the tooth. "Very well. I suppose you have done well for yourself. Your family may live."

"Thank you, my—"

I took a dagger from my cloak and stabbed Diedre through the neck with it. She evaporated into dust in front of me. Such a clean way to die. No blood, no fuss. "Their life, for yours."

CHAPTER 46
CHELLE

I scratched Albie's head tenderly as we walked toward Oz. He had whimpered the whole way through the forest with Balor, until we reached the church and Red gave him a tincture to stop the pain.

"How is he?" Rose asked.

I rubbed his mouth where his tooth used to be. "He'll be okay, I think. He's missing a tooth, but he's a tough snake."

"He's as tough as his mother," Rose said, reaching out to pet Albie with me.

"We don't have to go with them," I said to Rose as we walked through the brush behind Red and Balor. I kept her far enough behind that we could have a private conversation, but close enough to prevent arousing suspicion.

"We promised," Rose replied. "Besides, we wouldn't be together right now if it wasn't for them."

"We wouldn't have been separated if it wasn't for them."

"You can leave if you want," Red said, turning back to me. "However, you'll never make it to the Obsidian Spindle without us."

"Is that a threat?" I asked, clenching my fists.

Red spun around, her cloak fluttering behind her. "It's not a threat. It's a statement of fact. You will never get across the Cursed Sea without us, and you'll never get into the Wicked Witch's throne room without our help, either. Since those are the only two ways to reach the Obsidian Spindle, you're out of options."

"Besides," Rose said, placing her hand in mine. "They helped us. They are helpful. What kind of people would we be if we didn't return the favor?"

"Alive people, Rose."

"Well, there's no guarantee of that," Red said, moving forward down a steep embankment. "None of us are really alive or dead. Urgu is a weird middle ground."

"Rose is alive right now," I replied, joining her in sliding down the hill. "But I don't know for how long."

The brush cleared at the bottom of the hill, and we found ourselves in a massive valley. We had been walking uphill most of the evening, so the flat surface was a welcome relief. In the distance, rising out of the plains, was a sparkling city jutting into the sky like a bouquet of green, glass stalagmites. Hundreds of jeweled shards, hundreds of feet high, pointed into the air.

"That's Oz," Balor said. "Worst place you'll ever want to go. Beautiful, though. I'll give it that."

"What makes it so bad?" Rose asked.

"The queen," Red replied. "She has tainted every good thing about that place. She and Hera have expelled or executed everybody who doesn't agree with them, leaving nothing but sycophants and psychopaths left in their court. It is evil wrapped in beauty. Those who remain desire power above all else and are willing to sell their soul to get it, quite literally."

"They are all in service to Hera," Rose said.

"That's right. They have exchanged what remained of their will for the promise of eternal glory at Hera's side. Now come. There's a long way to go."

"I don't like this," I said.

"You're a baby," Rose said, falling back in step with me. "What could go wrong?"

"Everything. Literally everything."

"Then at least we'll have each other."

CHAPTER 47
RED

Children.

They were both children.

Children that would surely get us all dusted before the end.

The gorgon, though. She did love Rose. She'd proven it to me. That was something, I guess.

Of course, I could not possibly let her meet Ozma looking like a hideous monster. Ozma, for all her grace and understanding, would never accept a monster into her confidence. Luckily, I knew a dealer in magical artifacts who owed me a couple dozen favors.

Nearby, there was a small inn run by one of Balor's cousins, another shape shifter, who could help us fix our problem while giving us some desperately needed rest. I hated rest, but in six hundred years I still hadn't convinced my soul that it didn't need sleep.

It was near midnight when we finally reached the inn. The place was nothing special, except that it existed in the middle of the harsh mountains surrounding Oz, and that by itself was a feat. The inn was humble and small, but clean, and sturdy in its construction.

"Wait outside," I told Chelle and Rose before I walked with Balor toward the shop, which also acted as the lobby for the inn. There were not many travelers on the mountain pass, but almost everyone that traveled the path needed supplies and rest when they reached the inn.

"Do you really think this girl is the light that was promised?" Balor said under his breath. "She seems kind of naïve to me to be the prophesied one."

"Of course she's naïve," I grumbled. "She has no idea what she's in for, or what she's capable of. Neither of them do."

"Do you think Ozma will really take them to the Spindle if they help us?"

I paused at the front door of the inn. "I don't care, frankly. I am compelled to bring the girl to Queen Ozma so that she can regain a sense of hope for the future of Urgu. That is my place in the grand scheme. The rest of the prophesy has little to do with me. I am just the Bearer. If I had to guess, though, I would say Ozma will never let them leave this place." I looked back at the two girls. "Besides, if the prophesy is true, then they won't live to see the Return, even if they are the harbingers of it."

"That's too bad. They seem nice."

"What are two lives sacrificed against all of Urgu, and all of humanity?"

Balor sighed. "It doesn't make it any less sad."

I opened the door to the store. "I never said it wouldn't be sad when you joined me. I said together we would end this reign of terror. And we will, no matter what it takes. I made a promise to you once, and I intend to keep it."

"And get back in the good graces of Ozma."

I slapped his shoulder. "We will save her, and be welcomed back, my friend."

The store was filled with odds and ends, bits and bobbins. There were clothes and blankets, and cured meats, plus weapons and tools to get through the harsh winters. I walked past all of it and made straight for the counter where a slight, old woman with a pronounced hunch bent over the counter, cleaning it with a collection of feathers.

"Dilif, my cousin," Balor boomed. "You look so feeble."

The woman looked up and smiled. Half of her teeth had fallen out, and those that remained were rotted through. "Better than looking like you."

They stared at each other for a moment, eyeing each other from nose to naval. Then, they laughed and embraced.

"It's good to see you," Balor bellowed.

Dilif released Balor and pushed back from him. "Oh, if only I could say the same. Unfortunately, you only come when you need something."

"That's not true."

Dilif looked at him side eyed. "When was the last time you graced my door?"

Balor thought for a moment, trying to hide his shame. "A century or so ago."

Dilif crossed her arms. "And was it to say hello, or because you needed something?"

"That's not fair," Balor said breathlessly. "You know—the circumstances—"

There was a long silence. Dilif looked at Balor with hard eyes, but over a long moment, they softened. "I'm just kidding, my dear cousin. You still can't take a joke."

Balor's smile widened. "And you still can't tell one. A hundred years is too long."

"It's hard to believe it's been so long."

Balor nodded. "The month Hypnos vanished, give or take, marked it a hundred years this week that I last saw you, cousin."

Dilif groaned. "Yes, I will trust your memory. I try not to think about it. What can I do for you?"

"We were wondering if you had any magical amulets or other artifacts," I said.

Dilif scoffed. "Of course I do. Wouldn't be much of an alchemist if I didn't have magic like that, Red. What are you looking for?"

I pointed out the window. "Something to disguise that gorgon."

Dilif followed my gaze. When she saw the gorgon, she smiled. "Why would you want to hide her? She's beautiful."

"Perhaps, but she will stick out in Oz. You know the rules about bringing monsters within its borders."

Dilif turned back. "I do. The queen keeps powerful magic to guard against enchantments. Luckily for you, I'm the best and quickest alchemist in all of Urgu."

"So you have something that we can use to disguise her?"

Dilif shook her head. "Not on me. That kind of magic is old and costly. Not much need for disguise up here. You can be who you are, no matter what anybody else thinks." She paused for a moment, then said, "I only make items like that on request."

"What is it going to cost me?"

"Two flights and a heroic adventure."

I grumbled. "That's highway robbery."

She shrugged and resumed her dusting. "You're welcome to go to another alchemist. I think there's one on the other side of the valley. Seven hundred miles away."

I reached into my purse and pulled out a handful of dreams. I picked one up and examined it. Inside, the pink hues swirled and eddied until I saw the makings of a sea voyage. I placed it on the table and picked up another. It was of a woman baking a cake. Not that one. The next one was of somebody flying through the clouds, as was the next.

"These are my three most powerful dreams," I said, handing them to Dilif. "This better work."

Dilif cradled the dreams in her hands. "These girls must be very special for you to spend dreams like this."

I looked back out the window at Chelle and Rose. "You have no idea."

CHAPTER 48
ROSE

I knew Chelle was worried about me. She had come so far to save me. The thing was, and I would never admit it to her, I was having the time of my life. I never got to go on adventures. My whole life was the droll monotony of work, school, and worrying if I was going to die. So, being out in the country with my girlfriend, not having to care about whether I was about to go into a diabetic coma because I was already in one, was simply lovely.

"We could stay here, you know?" I said as I rested my head against Chelle's shoulder. We were snuggled up on a log in front of the alchemist's general store.

"Everybody here is miserable."

"Everybody at home is miserable."

"That's true, but at least they have bodies back home, and don't disappear into dust when they die."

It was a lovely, picturesque view over Oz. The sun rolled across the horizon and felt like I was looking at a Monet painting. Perhaps this what was the image people thought of when they painted perfection. Birds chirped and the wind blew through my hair. Albie slithered down onto my cheek and I reached up to pet him. When I did, Chelle cooed along with the snake. It was the best.

"How are you feeling, Albie?" I asked, scratching the snake's chin.

"He feels fine," Chelle said. "He'll feel better when we're home."

"When—we're home," I sighed. The more I thought about home, the more I dreaded it.

"Come on," Red said, stomping out of the store we'd been waiting outside of for hours. "Here." She tossed a necklace over to Chelle, who grabbed it, knocking me off her shoulder in the process.

"What is it?"

"It's another concealment necklace. Just like the one she used to wear."

A concealment necklace. As if Chelle wasn't good enough as she was? No way. I wasn't about to stand for her disguising herself.

"She doesn't have to wear that," I said. "She's not a freak to be hidden away."

Chelle clenched the necklace in her hand. "Rose, enough. It's not worth it."

"Yes," I said, stomping forward. "It is worth it. You are no better than everybody who freaked out at Chelle when she was growing up. Do you know how hard it is to be a monster on Earth?"

"No," Red said. "But I know how hard it is to be one here."

"Me too, girl," Balor added. "We can't get within five miles of Oz with her looking like that. Guards will dust her for even trying. It's not fair, but it's the truth."

"The truth sucks," I snapped.

"It does," Chelle said.

When I turned around, Chelle already had the necklace around her neck. She was no longer her gorgon self, but fully human, with dark skin and green eyes. She was as beautiful as ever, but I wished she didn't have to hide herself.

"You don't—"

"Stop," Chelle said, standing up. "Your privilege is showing."

"What's that supposed to mean?"

"It means you don't know what it's like to be a monster in the world. You don't get to make decisions for me. I don't like being different. I just want to blend in, and if this is helping me blend in, fine. It's not perfect, but it's something." She turned to Red. "How do I look?"

Red nodded. "Completely human."

I hated it.

CHAPTER 49
NIMUE

I sat across from my magic mirror, watching the gorgon slip on the necklace. The tooth Diedre handed over allowed me to form a bond between the mirror and the snake's eyes. Everything it saw, I saw, too.

It was a very good disguise. However, the snake still existed beneath it, masked from view, which meant I could see everything. Credit was due to the creator of the charm. They were quite skilled. Or perhaps, I would burn her cottage to the ground and take her for my own means.

Yes, that sounded like more fun. I would make a point to tell the generals about it.

There was a sudden flash in the room, and out of the light, a swirling cloud of smoke molded into the goddess Hera. Her skin was flawless and nearly translucent in its whiteness. Her eyes shone a bright purple. She wore a long, black toga, having long foregone her traditional white.

"Goddess!" I said, kneeling before her. I did not like to grovel, but she could snap me out of existence with merely a thought. I had no other choice but to avoid any degree of petulance and bow to her power. She was vindictive and petty, destroying whole civilizations for an imagined slight.

"Where is my dreamer?" Hera said. "Has she slipped through your fingers yet again?

I looked up at her, careful not to catch her eye. "We are narrowing in on her. Any moment we—"

Hera sneered. "You have disappointed me for too long. Perhaps it is time to find another."

I shook my head. "No. Look." I pointed to the mirror. "She comes to us. Soon, she will be within the confines of the Emerald City and we will have her without expending our army to find her."

Hera smiled. "Very good."

"And on top of that, she brings the Red Rider, and they head for Ozma."

"Ozma!" Hera said. "We can finally destroy that insolent cur, then?"

"That is my plan, my exalted one. I just need more time."

Hera looked down on me, her purple eyes searing into me. The longer they looked at me, the hotter I became, until it was sweating profusely under my collar.

"You have time, but not much. If the prophesy is correct, then Hypnos will return soon. We must snuff out our enemies before that happens."

"It will be done."

Hera walked toward the mirror, releasing me from her gaze. "Imagine, we can end Hypnos, the Ozma threat, and return to the universe all with the help of one little girl. Amazing, isn't it?"

"Yes, my god. That is my plan."

Hera turned to me. "Make sure it's done right this time."

She snapped her fingers and was gone. I dropped to the ground and took in a deep breath, happy to have survived one more encounter with the fickle god.

CHAPTER 50

RED

The Emerald City started its life five thousand years ago, as a simple castle—Hypnos's castle. It was the first thing that existed in Urgu, after the land itself, and the Obsidian Spindle, which predated Hypnos's rule by millions of years. The Fates had spent their days weaving threads since the dawn of time. They even spun the fates of the immortal gods.

That was what made them so powerful. The Dream Realm was a dangerous place to imprison displaced gods, but Zeus and Osiris trusted the Fates, and gave them the power to decide with whom they granted an audience. Hypnos quickly earned their trust and became a confidant. He understood the significance of the Fates, and that they needed absolute autonomy to do their work.

He filled the sea around the Spindle with unspeakable monsters to prevent anyone from travelling there, and he placed the entrance to the only bridge in his throne room. Only he or his chosen ruler had access. Those that wanted to parlay with the Fates without his blessing would have to brave the dangers within the Cursed Sea.

I chose the sea when I made my sojourn to the Spindle. There was a narrow strait where the distance between the Urgu main continent and the Spindle's island was at its smallest. I rowed out, certain that I would be eaten alive by the Kraken or dragged down into the depths by the mermaids.

I wasn't, though. I made it across and climbed the sheer rock face to the top of the Spindle. There, the Fates granted me an audience. I did not think I was worthy enough to see them, but they saw something in me. My bravery, maybe; my foolhardy bravery.

I begged them to send me back to Earth, but they told me that my body had died some months ago. There was no place there for me. I could not return to another body, and the Fates could not bring my body back from the dead. I was stuck in Urgu until I turned to dust. They allowed me another wish, but I had no other wish aside from returning to my life.

And so, I asked them to make me useful. They turned me into the Red Rider. Everything I have done since then was not of my own control, but divine intervention. I do not feel agency for my actions but a compulsion to protect my queen and to save the realm. I felt a sense of duty deep in the depth of my hollow soul, as if something beyond my control pulled me against my will to perform some task or another, always putting me in the right place at the right time.

That was how I knew that I was doing the right thing. Dragging Rose and Chelle across the rocks and past the cadre of guards patrolling Oz's wall made me feel useful. Soon, Ozma would see the prophesy was real, and thank me for my service. That would also make me useful. Eventually, she would be back on the throne, and we would have a rightful heir. That would make me useful.

It took another half a day of hiking to reach the border of Oz. The walls of the Emerald City were higher than when Hypnos built them a million years ago, and now they were far more splendid. The glass walls protecting Oz Emerald City glistened in the sun like perfectly polished gems. That was by design. No army could look on the Emerald City and not go blind, Ozma once told me. It protected them from every invasion. Except a coup from within, of course.

"How much further?" Rose asked as we climbed a rock embankment.

"We're almost there," I replied. "We have to be careful to avoid detection. If anyone sees us climbing around the back of Oz, they'll hang us for sure."

Above me, the great bridge that connected the throne room to the Obsidian Spindle loomed large. Embedded in its smooth face, a million opals sparkled in a thousand different colors in the light of day. In the distance, across the Cursed Sea, the Obsidian Spindle rose like a gnarled and burnt willow trunk.

Below the Spindle and the bridge, the Cursed Sea called out, beckoning travelers into its murky deep. Past the Spindle was the edge of the world. Nothing existed beyond its walls, except the invisible barrier which kept us from Earth, and inside the Spindle laid the only way back to Earth.

I pulled Rose up the jagged glass wall that protected the Emerald City from invasion, and then did the same for Chelle. The glass was difficult to climb and left cuts everywhere, but it prevented an invasion from the rear and allowed for only a skeleton force to protect Oz from the seaward side.

Protecting that seaward side of Oz was the lowest job a soldier could have in the queen's army. The combination of lack of skill and dearth of overall numbers made it easy to navigate the back of Oz by foot without being detected.

Most people entered the great city from the front. Some people, however, knew about the underground network of secret passageways which connected the Emerald City to the rest of the world. Nobody used them. Created by Hypnos, he told his chosen about them. Ozma knew them all, but Nimue was oblivious.

When Ozma left the Green Palace, her first hiding place was under the city, right in the shadow of the Wicked Witch. She stayed there for thirty nights to gather those loyal to her. Not many came down to join her. Many of those loyal to Ozma had been slaughtered, and of those who remained, most didn't care who was in charge, as long as they could keep power.

"Up ahead," I whispered to the others. I eyed Balor, who scuttled ahead closer to the walls to act as a lookout. He waved us forward, and I scampered forward with the others.

"Where is this place?" Chelle asked.

"There is a crypt under Oz for the first kings of Hypnos. It holds the ashes of those fallen before Ozma's reign. It was once hundreds of miles outside the castle. However, as the castle grew, the city abutted it, but the catacombs have remained a secret."

"How do you know she's here?" Rose asked. "How can the stars in a church tell you how to find the queen?"

"Each star in that temple we visited is the location of a secret base of Ozma. Everyone in Ozma's charge must memorize it. The star on Hypnos's forehead is this crypt, because it is at the seat of his power, and a secret from those who wish the crown harm. She often comes back here, even against the advice from her council, to be near the throne, and her home."

I caught up with Balor and together we ran to the glass wall that surrounded Oz. Along the ground were a series of craggy black rocks. Placing my hand on the ground, I traced my finger along the dirt until I found a groove in a large, black rock. I brushed off the sand and sure enough, there was the symbol of Oz. A sleeping moon hidden behind a cloud, made from the letters O and Z. I pressed my palm on the symbol and it gave way. Beneath me, the ground rumbled, and I dove out of the way as it opened below me, revealing a passageway.

"Come on."

I pulled a pink dream out of my money purse. Dreams did not give off much light, but they worked in a pinch. The light pink hue bounced off the walls. I watched the others descend into the ground, and then the chasm closed behind them.

"This is spooky," Rose said.

"*Ignium*," Chelle whispered and her hand lit up with a small flame. "Better?"

"Much."

We reached the bottom of a stairwell that opened up into a large room lined with small boxes. The boxes had gathered dust in the centuries since they were placed here, but inside each were the ashes of a great king of Oz. On each wall was a burning torch, and in the middle was a young woman with golden hair, dressed in green, wearing a crown of tree bark, with eyes as blue as ice.

"Ozma," I said, dropping to my knees.

"Gabrielle," Ozma replied. "Welcome home."

CHAPTER 51
CHELLE

The crypts were dark and dusty, except for the few flickering torches and the fire from my hands. We ended up in a big room, with some weird kid wearing a crown of tree bark, and she called Red by the name Gabrielle. I hated everything about Urgu, but there was little I hated more than these crypts. They were cramped and impossible to fight in, and there was only one method of escape, a staircase.

"My queen," Red said, genuflecting.

"It's good to see you, Ozma," Balor said. He also bowed low.

Really? Ozma was nothing but a little child. She couldn't have been more than fifteen years old.

"You may stand," Ozma said to Red, who obliged. "You risked much to come here. The last time we spoke I banished you to the far reaches of the kingdom."

"That was so long ago."

"Twenty years, almost to the day, and yet it feels like yesterday to me."

"Excuse me?" Rose said. "You said you were working for Ozma."

Red looked back at her. "I am working for Ozma. She didn't approve of my quest, but I did it for her."

A lie. Typical. I knew I couldn't trust her. "So, you are a liar, then?"

"I'm not a liar," Red said. "I just didn't unpack the whole truth. Ozma frowned upon my search for the chosen one, but I knew it was the answer to everything."

"Which is where we differ," Ozma replied with a hint of contempt bouncing on her voice. "I had more pragmatic concerns, like staying alive."

"Which you have done," Red said. "Even without my protection."

"I have become...wily since we last spoke. Before you left, you said that I wouldn't last a week without you to protect me."

"And I was gleefully wrong, but where is your council? And your guards?"

"They are few and scattered to the wind. One day, they will rejoin me, when the time is right." Ozma turned toward Rose. "And who is this?"

I pushed forward to block Rose from view. I spoke harshly. "You can stay back, please...queen."

"You don't speak that way to Queen Ozma!" Balor shouted.

I held up my hand, which was still on fire. "I just did."

Ozma stepped forward and smiled at me. She leaned down to my hand and with a light exhale, the fire in my hand went out. "I like you."

"How did you do that?"

"I do not have the full power of Hypnos, but his blessing still runs through my veins."

"You can use magic?" Rose said.

"Little more than parlor tricks these days, really. Since Hypnos left, my power has waned."

"That's why we're here, my queen," Red said, taking a step toward Rose. I gave her a dirty look but didn't stop her. "This is Rose. She's a dreamer. A new one. She came into Urgu through the portal just like dreamers did when Hypnos was still here."

"She did?" Ozma replied breathlessly.

"That's right. Exactly one hundred years since Hypnos's disappearance, just like the prophesy said."

Ozma chuckled. "You and that prophesy. When will you accept that the Fates left us here to rot? They don't want to help us. They want to see us suffer. I don't believe a word they ever said. If they wanted to help us, they would have opened their doors to me years ago instead of watching everything I care about turn to dust."

"You should. Because it's true. Just like I said. I wasn't giving you false hope. I just needed time. But this is proof. Hypnos is still alive, and with this girl's help, we can bring him back."

"And exactly how do you do that?" Chelle said.

Red looked down at the ground. "I'm not sure...yet. But that's why I brought you to Ozma. She's the wisest person in Urgu."

"She's a child!" I shouted.

"Only in stature," Ozma said softly. "I'm three thousand and twenty years old."

I blinked a few times. I was not expecting this information. "Well, then. You look good for your age."

Ozma's gaze fell on me for a long, silent moment as she studied every crevice of my face. "Who is this?"

"That's...her girlfriend, Chelle."

"Fascinating," Ozma said. "And did you come through the portal as well?"

I shook my head. "No. I came here through a door guarded by Mydnyte."

"Interesting." Ozma pointed to my necklace. "Your enchantment. What does it mask?"

"I'd rather not say."

"Because you're ashamed?"

"She's not ashamed," Rose poked in. "She just doesn't want to freak you out."

"What does that mean?" Ozma said. "Freak out?"

"That you won't like it."

Ozma giggled. "My dear, I doubt anything can freak me out."

"It's because I'm a gorgon," I said.

"Incredible. And you thought I would not be okay with this?"

"I didn't know what you would think. I really didn't care, either. Red thought it would be better, and she knows this dumb place better than I do."

"Yes, there was a time when I was uneasy around monsters. However, if my exile has taught me anything, it's that there are no bad races, just bad people. I have relied on the kindness of all types in my time away from the throne."

"I like that story," Rose said with a smile. "Not the exile part, but the not being a bigoted jerk part."

"I like that part, too." Ozma turned away from us, her hand on her chin. "This is all fascinating. Thank you, Gabrielle. You have brought me something to ponder."

"Does that mean I can stay?" Red asked cautiously.

Ozma smiled. "Yes, it means you can stay. At least until we figure this all out."

"And I too?" Balor added.

Ozma turned away. "Both of you. For now, please, let me think on this in silence. I will be back to you shortly, or longly, depending on how long it takes to think."

I exhaled loudly and crossed my arms. "I don't mean to be rude, but none of this is why we're here."

"Oh?" Ozma said, spinning back around.

"We're here to get to the Obsidian Spindle and get back home. That's it. I don't know or care about a prophesy."

Ozma looked me up and down. "No, you wouldn't, would you? After all, you have no idea the depth of our struggle."

"I'm sorry. I feel bad I don't feel bad, but we just want to go home."

"Very well," Ozma said. "If that is your wish, I will send you across the Cursed Sea on a boat within the hour."

"You can't!" Red said. "They have to help us."

Ozma shook her head. "They don't have to do anything. They

must help of their own free will. Otherwise, we are monsters, just as bad as Nimue."

"So, we can just go?" I asked. "Just like that?"

She nodded. "Just like that."

I looked back at Rose, who glared at me. I could tell what she was thinking, but I didn't care. My job was to get her back home, not to be a savior to a forgotten realm.

"Tell me, though," Ozma said. "What did you promise Mydnyte to get her to open the door to Urgu? She is not known to be persuaded easily."

My jaw clenched. "I told her I would kill Hera."

Ozma chuckled. "And yet, that was a lie?"

I nodded, slowly and carefully. "That's right."

Ozma smiled broadly as she stared deeply into my eyes. "You really are quite interesting, and bold. I could have used one like you."

I broke away from her gaze. "I'm sorry to disappoint you."

She shook her head. "You aren't a disappointment. I don't even know you well enough to decide whether you would help or hurt me. I suppose I'll never know, and there is some relief in that. I already have enough to worry about. Worrying that you would betray me, or turn away from me, or not fulfill your promise is not something I need to add. So, in some ways, I should thank you."

"You're...welcome?"

Rose swallowed loudly. "Won't Urgu be doomed if we don't help you, though? What about the prophesy?"

"We have survived for a hundred years without Hypnos. This world will keep spinning without him for another century, even if it's not as perfect as we would like."

CHAPTER 52
ROSE

"You shouldn't leave," Red said. We were sitting on the stairs of the catacombs. Chelle was out procuring a boat for us to use to cross the lake and forbade me from leaving the crypt until she returned. She had never forbidden me from doing anything before. I wasn't somebody who liked being forbade from doing things, even if it was out of love.

"I don't want to leave. I actually like it here."

Red looked up at me. "Then why are you going to leave? You can stay here, help us defeat Nimue, and bring Ozma back to the throne."

As I considered my response, Chelle called down the stairs, "Come on. We can go now."

I stood up and faced her. "What if I don't want to go?"

"We already talked about that."

"No, we didn't. You talked about it for me. You never asked what I wanted. I like it here, Chelle. I've never liked it anywhere before. Nobody ever wanted me somewhere like these people do."

Chelle took a step down onto the stairs. "Yeah, and what happens when they use you in some stupid experiment, or they find out you aren't the chosen one? You'll go back to being a nothing burger to them. And then you'll be stuck here. In this place, with nothing."

"No, she won't," Red said. "She's not a nothing burger, whatever that is. She's the chosen one."

"I know you say that, but I grew up hearing stories about chosen ones. The ones who came to steal from my people, enslave my people, kill my people, so I'm not so fond of chosen ones, truth be told."

"Is that why you want us to leave?" I asked softly.

Chelle shook her head. "No, sweetie. It's because this place is a fantasy. It's not the real world."

"It's real for these people."

Chelle took my hands in hers. "These people are living in the past. Look at them. It's been thousands of years and they haven't figured out cars, or planes, or even running water. Romans had running water, Rose, and this place is older than that. You ever think about why they don't have any of that stuff?"

"They have computers, at least some sort of computers."

"Yeah, and how did they use it? To hurt you. To kill people."

Red piped up, "And it's different on Earth? They use their technology to kill people there, too, from what I remember."

"Stay out of this," Chelle said. She looked at me again, touched my face. "This isn't real, Rose. None of this is real. Don't you get that?"

I felt a little ashamed. I hadn't thought about any of that stuff, honestly. "What if I don't want real? What if real sucks?"

She shrugged. "At least it is real."

"This is all nonsense." Red stepped between us. "If Rose wants to stay, then you should allow her to stay."

"No," I said. I actually stomped my feet. "Nobody *allows* me to do anything. Chelle, I love you, but you're being a real bitch."

Chelle sighed. "I'm sorry." She took my hands. "I'm just trying to protect you."

"I don't need protecting. I need a partner." I slipped my hands out of hers. "Somebody to walk with, not behind."

Chelle bit her lip. "I can't stay here, Rose. It's not my place. I need you to come with me back to Earth. I know you think I'm brave, but I'm not. You make me strong. I don't know what I would do if I lost you."

"You may have already lost me. What if we get to the Spindle and find out I'm dead? What if the Fates won't let us in?"

"Then we'll figure it out, but that hasn't happened yet. We can still go home right now. Home, Rose. Where we belong."

I dropped my head. "I'm not sure it's where I belong."

"I thought you belonged with me?" Chelle said, her voice wavering. She sniffed.

"And I thought you belonged with me." I loved her more than anything, but she hated it here. I couldn't force her to stay here, even if it was what I wanted. "But I'll go with you. I love you, and one of us has to sacrifice. I'll do it, because I love you."

"Gross." Red was staring at us with her arms folded across her chest, tapping her foot.

"Shut up," Chelle said to her, without taking her eyes off me. "We're going to make it work. It's going to be great."

I wasn't sure she was right, but maybe being in love wasn't about getting whatever you want. Maybe it was about making you both happy, even if that meant going against every bone in your body telling you to do something different.

"Thank you," Chelle said, curling her fingers around mine, and for the first time since we met, I had to force myself not to pull back from her when she leaned in to kiss me.

It will be okay, I thought. As long as we're together, everything will be fine.

CHAPTER 53
CHELLE

I didn't want to tell Rose that I knew what was best for her, but I knew what was best for her. The Dream Realm was just that—a dream. A silly dream that she would eventually wake from and realize that she didn't have a body, or the ability to get back to Earth.

I didn't know what happened if you died when you weren't asleep, but it had to be better than Urgu with its petty sniping and wicked witches.

"Come on," I said, leading Rose down to the beach below the jagged glass wall, away from Oz. Balor and I found a small rowboat and took painstaking efforts to line it up at the smallest part of the sea, just like Red had done so many years ago. "You'll feel better when we're across the sea."

"Will I?" Rose asked. "I hope so, because I don't feel so good about leaving right now."

I pointed across the sea to the Obsidian Spindle, where it spiraled high into the sky, broken and crooked like Bellatrix Lestrange's wand. "That's home, okay? I know you don't like Earth right now, but at least there you still have a body. You still have a choice. I promise it's going to get better once we're back."

"When?" Rose said. "When is it going to get better?"

I didn't have an answer, so instead I helped Rose into the boat. I could still make out the Emerald City in the distance. The coastline was a crescent shape, with Oz being the furthest point in the center.

"Just because yer at the smallest crossing point of the sea doesn't mean the crossing's going to be easy," Balor said to me as I hopped into the boat.

"I know that," I replied without looking at him.

He clenched the side of the boat. "I wish ya'd reconsider. We could really use your help."

I shook my head. "I came here with a mission, and I intend to see it through."

"Even if it's not what Rose wants?"

"She doesn't know what she wants," I snapped. I sat down and picked up the oars. "Just kick us off, okay?"

Balor didn't say another word. He shoved hard and we floated into the sea. I started to paddle, but the water was dark like oil and gooey like sludge. It was hard to make headway. With every stroke a moan blared from the water, as if it were alive and we were hurting it. Balor had told me horror stories about the cursed lake, and of the mermaids who roamed the deep, waiting to feed on brave travelers.

I had never met a mermaid before, but knew about them from my mother, who told me stories of them dragging travelers down to the depths. I had no intention of being dragged into the depths.

"Hey," I said, smiling at Rose. "It will all be over soon."

"And then what?" Rose sighed. "Then, I'll go back to being a nothing burger from nowhere."

"It's not so great being wanted. It's more trouble than it's worth."

"Seemed pretty cool from where I sat."

A stiff breeze gusted across the water, and the oars jerked violently in the sea. I lifted them from the water, and noticed a long, jagged claw mark in the left one. The mermaids knew we were here. They were coming for us. I would have to use magic to cross the sea.

Most of my magic was defensive or offensive in nature, but I had practiced a propulsion spell with my mother.

Before I could say the words, a familiar screech came from above us. I recognized the sound from our time in the woods. It was a dragon. A moment later, it ducked below the cloud cover and dive-bombed for us. The dragon was enormous, even from a hundred feet in the air.

"*Aqua scutum!*" I shouted and the water rose from the lake to create a shield around us. The dragon slammed into the shield and rose higher into the air. I held the shield in the air with one arm and pointed behind the boat with the other.

"*Jet aquae!*" The water above me fell back into the sea and began to move behind us, creating a turbine like we had a motor.

The dragon divebombed again. "*Aqua scutum!*"

I cast another shield with my free hand, but it was nowhere as potent as the last. I didn't have the strength to maintain both spells, and the dragon was too powerful. With its third dive, the dragon broke the shield apart and slammed straight into the boat, throwing it into the air.

"Rose!" I shouted as I was thrown into the water.

I sunk down into the black sludge. Below the surface, a hundred glowing blue eyes stared at me, closing in on me as I descended into the deep. Mermaids. They were not kind or beautiful like the movies say, but heinous and deformed. They had hideous scales down their bodies and their webbed feet propelled them in the water faster than I could evade them. I used what remained of my strength to swim up to the surface. It was like swimming through quicksand. Before the creatures could catch me, I broke through the plain of the water.

I took a deep breath, inhaling water. A dozen small claws grappled with my legs. "*Tutela bulla!*" I shouted before I fell back under the water. Instantly, the bubble formed around me, knocking the mermaids away from me. Floating inside the bubble, I crested back to the surface and swam to the boat.

"Rose! Rose!"

I grabbed onto the side of boat and heaved myself up. But Rose and the dragon were both gone.

CHAPTER 54
RED

Livid was an apt word to describe how I felt. Ozma let Rose and Chelle go without even putting up a fight. I had worked for a hundred years to find a person capable of fulfilling the prophesy, and Ozma just let them walk right out.

I had been stewing about it and pacing furiously. I couldn't take it anymore. I stormed into Ozma's chamber, where she was sitting cross-legged in calm silence, candles flickering. "Why did you do it?" I barked.

"Do what?" Ozma said, not even flinching. She lit a stick of incense.

"Why did you let them go?"

Ozma looked up at me. "Because we are not monsters, Gabrielle. We can't force people to fight with us if they don't want to."

"But Rose wanted to stay. You could have convinced her."

"Perhaps. She chose to go, no matter her reasons. If she is the chosen one, she will return."

I wanted to yell but something caught my eye. Ozma had surrounded herself in a circle of ash and with exactly six candles equidistant around her.

"You're praying to the old gods."

"I am. One of them, at least."

"So, you do believe that he is still out there, somewhere?"

"I believe that I would not have my powers if Hypnos was gone from this plane of existence. However, where he is, I still cannot discern. Not even after all this time." She sighed.

The temple shook and quaked underneath us. I heard rocks shifting in front of the temple and a thin shaft of light came from above the stairs. Something was coming to us. Perhaps it was Rose coming back, having thought better of herself. I rushed to the front with eager anticipation, only to be met by the clanking armor of the Wicked Witch's soldiers.

"You will pay for this trespass," I snarled.

I pulled out my daggers and sliced at the soldiers sprinting toward me. Their armor was only susceptible to attack in three places, but after a thousand encounters, I knew those places well. I placed my strikes on the left side of the abdomen and under the arm.

The first two soldiers I dusted without trouble, but there were more coming down. Dozens more. I feared I couldn't hold them back.

"Ozma!" I screamed and a moment later she appeared.

She clapped her hands together and pushed them apart, extending her arms toward the soldiers. A burst of fire came from her hands. She closed her eyes and used her mind to fling the clay pots from the shelf. They shattered, dispelling their ashes into the air, the last remnants of their existence.

"Go!" Ozma screamed.

"I'm not leaving you!"

"Yes, you are!" She placed her hands on me and whispered to herself. "Find me in the dungeon." She snapped her fingers and I was gone into the wind. The last thing I saw was a half dozen soldiers descend on her as she collapsed to the ground.

CHAPTER 55
CHELLE

By the time I dragged myself onto shore, I was a soggy mess. I had been swimming for gods knew how long. The muddy water made moving horribly slow, and with every stroke of my arms the mermaids tried to pop the bubble which protected me from them. It took what remained of my will, but I had survived. Now I had to find Rose.

"Are you okay?" Balor said. He came running up to me from the beach and supported me as I pushed up to my knees.

I coughed water into the sand. "No. What happened? Where did that dragon come from?"

"I don't know." He helped me stand up. "I was headed back to Ozma when I saw the dragon. It came on you two like lightning. I rushed back to help, but by the time I had, you were under water and the beast had carried Rose away. I stayed on shore in case there was another attack, but none came back for you. Perhaps you are not very important."

"Thanks."

There was a brilliant flash of light in front of us. Red jumped out of it and slammed onto the ground. She pushed to her feet, daggers in hand, and screamed like a ferocious and untethered beast.

"Ozma!" she shouted.

"Quiet, child!" Balor said. "You'll wake the dead."

Red lunged forward when she saw me. "You. It's you. What have you done?"

"Me? I didn't do anything. Rose was just captured by a dragon. What did you do to her?"

"Nothing! I did—wait. Let me see you closer." She grabbed at my face.

"Get off me!"

"Hold still," Red stepped forward and peered deep into my left eye, then my right. Dissatisfied with what she found, she turned her attention up onto my head and studied each snake on my head, until she grabbed onto Albie and pulled him close to her.

"Ow!" I shouted. "Get off of him. He's been through enough!"

"I know the Eye of Hera is upon you." Red dove into one of the purses on her belt and pulled out a yellow tonic. "Drink this."

"No!" I shouted. "I don't—"

Red squeezed Albie tighter, and I dropped to my knees. "If you want to get Rose back, do as I say."

I took the tonic and downed it. It tasted like warm piss. Once I swallowed it all a scream filled my ears until I heard a glass shatter inside my body. A shockwave went through me, and I collapsed to the ground.

"What happened?" I said, trying to stand.

"The Wicked Witch found a piece of you and used it to make a connection between your snake and her magic mirror. It's a simple spell to counter, or prevent outright, but you are so new she must have realized you would not be immune to it."

"So, she saw..."

"Everything you saw, and it led her right to Ozma, and Rose."

"What do we do now?" I asked, rising to my feet.

"We get them back," Red said with a snarl.

"That's suicide," Balor said.

Red glared. "Only if we fail."

"Aye, that's why I said it."

"Then we won't fail," I growled. "Whatever you need, I'm in. Let's take this witch down."

CHAPTER 56
NIMUE

My precious dragon shrieked as it flew toward me carrying the two prizes I had commanded it to retrieve. The dreamer for Hera, and the gorgon for me. Dragons rarely let me down. However, when it perched on my balcony, it dropped the dripping wet and unconscious dreamer at my feet. There was no sign of the monster.

"Where is the other one?" I asked. "The gorgon?" I didn't know why I bothered asking it. Even if I could control dragons, I couldn't understand them. "Imbecile. Find her!"

The dragon spread its wings and flew away to find my monstrous prize. I ran to my magic mirror. "Mirror, Mirror on the wall. Find me the gorgon child."

The mirror flipped between a hundred colors in a couple of seconds, but then it went black. I knew what had happened. There was only one thing a black mirror could have meant. The red brat had found my gorgon and dispelled my power.

"Drat," I mumbled to myself.

No matter. Soon Ozma would be in my clutches, and if I knew the Red Rider at all, she would come for them, and she would bring the gorgon directly to me. All I had to do was wait patiently, and that was one thing I knew how to do quite well. After all, I had bided my time for hundreds of years already. What was another couple of days measured against an eternity?

CHAPTER 57

RED

There was no way to get through the main gates of the Emerald City without somebody finding and capturing us. There was, however, a good chance that Nimue didn't know about the tunnel that led from the catacombs into the city. Ozma's spies had used it for years to learn the comings and goings of the Wicked Witch's movement.

If Nimue had discovered every secret passageway of Oz, then we were doomed. It was a risk I had to take—there wasn't any other choice. And this passageway would take us directly to the Cathedral of the six, right next door to the castle. It was our best chance to enter Nimue's sanctuary unnoticed.

To reach the catacomb passageway, we'd have to go through the crypts, which meant taking out the half dozen guards stationed there. "Okay," I said, ducking down next to Chelle and Balor behind one of the hills nearest the catacombs. "We should easily be able to take them out."

"I only count six."

"There are probably more in the tombs. Ozma had many secrets she kept hidden down there. Luckily, they'll be confined and easy to take out."

"You seem awfully confident about that," Balor chimed in.

I wasn't confident. I was terrified. For all I knew, there could be a hundred troops underground, waiting for us to pop our heads out before they attacked. However, that didn't change one truth.

"It's the best chance we have."

As I stood up to attack, five of the guards walked back into the tomb leaving the entrance guarded by only one person, but who knew how long they would be downstairs before they returned.

"If you think this is the best course forward, lass," Balor said, "then, I'm with you."

"And you?" I asked, turning to Chelle.

"I don't know this city well enough to have an opinion. I hate this plan, but if it's our best shot to save Rose, then let's do it."

I nodded. "Good. Then let's go."

The guard turned his back toward me as I crested the hill. I rushed toward him and lunged into the air. It was the only chance I had to strike, and I took it, leaping onto his back and digging my knife into his neck until he dusted into nothingness.

"Come on," I said to the others, gesturing for them to follow me.

I peered down into the cave. I only heard the low mumble of a few guards. I crept down the stairs silently, slowly, descending into the darkness. Two guards stood at the bottom of the stairs in the ashes of the fallen kings which Ozma had flung into the air in a desperate attempt to save me not long ago.

Ozma. She had to be all right. The false queen had hunted her for decades, and would relish her capture, savoring every moment and fighting the urge to kill her quickly. I needed to believe that. If Ozma was already dead, then all of Urgu was doomed.

I turned back to Balor and gave him a nod. Together, we ran forward and dusted the guards in the first room. Their ashes fell to the ground and mixed in with those from the royal line of Oz.

Chelle rushed past us and into the other door. She muttered something under her breath. The ash beneath her feet molded into a stake and she flung it into a guard's stomach, dusting him. We moved forward through the crypt, obliterating any guards that came in our way, until we reached a stone wall with the man in the moon and seal of Ozma's house on it.

I placed my hand on the nose of the moon and twisted it counterclockwise. It resisted me at first, but with a quick jerk of my wrist the nose clicked and spun. Once it made a full rotation, it disappeared into the face of the moon and the wall parted to reveal a long tunnel.

I beckoned the others forward. "This way."

"Duh," Chelle said, following me.

The minute our rescue attempt was over, I was going to punch her in the face. For the time being, an uneasy ally was better than none, especially one with magical powers. I had to put up with her, even if she irritated me enough that I happily fantasized about her death.

The corridor went on for longer than I remembered from the last time I'd used it, a century ago. Usually, the path was lit with torches like the catacombs. I didn't want to reveal our position in case anyone was in the darkness with us, so I did not light them. The path twisted and turned through the new city, and then into the mid-city, and finally into the Old City, where the castle was located.

A metal ladder, unused for years, sat against the wall and led to a trap door in the floor above. I had used it once to shuffle the rightful heir out of the castle and to safety, and now I used it to save her a second time.

"I don't know what we will find when we get above ground," I said to Chelle and Balor. "There might be a hundred guards waiting for us, or none. Be prepared for anything."

I grabbed onto the ladder and pulled myself up. At the top I unlatched the trap door and slowly pushed it open. The tunnel led into the Cathedral of the Six, the largest church in the whole of Urgu. There were many more churches dedicated to the Six, and temples to worship the individual gods, but none were as grand as the cathedral.

The secret passageway led into one of the confessionals. Only the high priest knew of it, and Nimue had murdered him in a show of force in the first days of her reign.

I pulled myself up onto the pew and walked out into the cathedral. A rainbow of lights came through the stained-glass windows that rose a hundred feet into the air. They depicted the Six as the church saw them, venerated and perfect, instead of flawed as I had come to know them.

Chelle walked out from behind me, eyeing the cathedral. "It's really something. I don't go for this hero worship shit, but this is pretty nice."

"It's something, all right. From a time before Hypnos abandoned Urgu and left it in the hands of Hera."

"They've reconstructed this old place five times," Balor added. "Every time a new god was imprisoned here, they added to it. First, as the church of Hypnos, and then Hypnos and Hera, then—"

"We get it," I grunted. "We're not here for a history lesson. Come. There is a secret entrance into the castle not far ahead. One that I doubt even the Wicked Witch has found yet. It's in a garden off the main street."

Chelle raised an eyebrow. "You make a lot of assumptions, don't you?"

I shrugged. "I follow my gut. It hasn't led me astray yet."

A gift from the Fates. My gut was never wrong, and it distrusted Chelle. I wasn't sure why just yet. I felt no ill will toward her, aside from the overwhelming desire to punch her in the mouth.

"That is literally not true," Chelle said. "Otherwise, we wouldn't be here."

I turned to her. "My only mistake was in trusting you. From the beginning, my gut has told me that you were trouble. I should have listened to it."

"Ladies," Balor said. "We can kill each other later, yes?"

I shot him a smile. "I look forward to that."

CHAPTER 58

ROSE

I was so sick of blacking out and waking up in strange places. The last thing I remembered was a giant dragon picking me up in its talons and lifting me into the air. I assumed I would be eaten, but it seemed as though Urgu had other plans for me.

"You're up," I heard from the shadows. "I thought you might be dead."

Out of the darkness stepped Ozma, still just as radiant as the last time I saw her, but without the smile that I remembered from our last encounter.

"Ozma!" I said breathlessly. "Where are we?"

"My castle, or more correctly, what used to be my castle. Unfortunately, it now belongs to Nimue. It is a sad state of affairs what has happened to us, but not one that was unforeseen. I always assumed that one day I would end up in this dungeon, unless Hypnos saw fit to return, which I knew was unlikely at best."

"You knew you would come here one day?"

Ozma sat down next to me. "I knew not when it would happen, but that it would happen. I could not run forever. My power was fading, and hers grows stronger with each passing day."

"That sucks."

"I don't know this expression."

"It means not very good."

"Oh. Well then yes, it sucks. It has sucked for one hundred years. That is why my Gabrielle has much hope for you, and why I had to cast her out."

"Why did you cast her out?"

"A rebellion is not built on hope, little one. It is built on what can be seen and done in the concrete, not the abstract. Gabriel fought against that idea and spent all her life talking about how we can get Hypnos back. It permeated my troops' consciousnesses. It made them sloppy. It made them overlook the truth. The false hope consumed my men, while I knew the truth…"

"And what is the truth?"

"Hypnos isn't coming back. Wherever he is, he will be there forever, and there was nothing we can do to find him. Instead, we must try to gain support from the other gods and take down Hera. Unfortunately, the gods are fickle, and their allegiances are hard won."

"The gods don't want to help?"

"Why would they help? They care nothing for Oz or Hera. They have their own games to play, and those plans don't involve helping me, a powerless refugee queen."

"That's horrible."

"It is neither good nor bad. It just is, child."

"It's funny, you look like a child."

"And yet, you are one. I have seen much in three millennia on Urgu. I watched my predecessor rise and fall, and the one before that and before that, until the mantle fell to me."

"Your parents?"

She shook her head. "That is not how the royal succession works in Urgu. You are chosen by Hypnos himself for your grace, determination, poise, and character, just like Hera has her champion, you become his. I suppose I am the last of his line."

"Because he abandoned you?"

"In a way, but I also failed him. I failed to prevent this takeover by Nimue, and I failed to keep him from being exiled."

"It's not your fault," I said. "Hera is an evil shrew."

Ozma chuckled. "Everyone in the royal court is the same, my dear. They are all heartless and vindictive. My job was to play their emotions and make them believe in our vision for the future. Unfortunately, it didn't take. Their allegiances turned to Nimue when I fell out of favor."

I didn't understand. "What vision?"

"Modernity," Ozma said. "We have been stuck in the past. We wanted to bring Urgu into the future. We heard tales of the Industrial Revolution on Earth. That was what I wanted here."

I scratched my head. "The only piece of technology I've seen around here was the computer terminal which was used to nearly kill me."

Ozma let out a deep sigh. "Yes, that was, sadly, a prototype of my design. Please believe me, it was meant to help humanity, not hurt it."

I moved toward her. "I do believe you."

"Thank you," Ozma said, solemnly. "I showed it to the royal council, and they called it heresy. That was the last straw for them. I believe that was the end of my reign, though it wouldn't officially end for some years hence."

I cocked my head. "And that's why they turned on you?"

"The main reason," Ozma said with a sad nod. "They also thought I was too kind to the peasants. Hypnos had love in his heart for all in Urgu, not just those in the royal class. We both knew the workers were being exploited, and that needed to end. Whenever you tell powerful men to cede their power, there will be trouble. Hypnos thought we could turn them, but we did not expect them to turn to Hera and pledge their loyalty to her, and to the Wicked Witch."

"How awful," I said, touching her shoulder gently. "We have to get you back on the throne."

"That's very kind of you," Ozma said, patting my hand with hers. "But you have made your decision to leave us and return to Earth. This is no longer your concern."

She was right. Damn Chelle for putting me in an impossible position. If I ever got out of here, she would convince me to go to the Obsidian Spindle, and home.

Wait. That was it. The Obsidian Spindle. I could still help.

"No. If we get into the Obsidian Spindle, I can change fate. I can change the Wicked Witch's fate. I could make this all right again."

"You only get one request of the Fates, Rose. You can't save us and save yourself at the same time. You must choose."

"Why?"

"That is part of being an adult. Nobody likes it, but that doesn't make it any less true."

"I hate it."

"Me too."

The door to the cell opened and a long-haired guard stepped inside. He snapped his fingers and two more came into the room and grabbed Ozma.

"Bring her."

"No!" I shouted, rushing to stop them. "Let her go."

The long-haired guard scoffed and slapped me down with his metal gauntlet. "You'll have your turn, welp. Enjoy your breaths while they still last."

But I wouldn't. I couldn't enjoy anything. Not while I knew Urgu would soon lose its rightful heir.

CHAPTER 59
NIMUE

Commander Balsim's men dragged Ozma into my throne room and threw her at my feet. A lot had changed since the days when she sat upon the throne. For one thing, I had turned her precious golden throne into one made of obsidian and onyx. I replaced her desire for perfection with my own twisted design honoring the chaos that reigns in us all.

"Welcome," I said to her with a smirk. "You are mighty hard to catch."

Ozma didn't look at me when she spoke. "I have long wondered what horrors you brought to the Great Hall."

I gestured to the room with a smirk. "Do you like it?"

Ozma demanded symmetry and order from everything, even her subjects, and that permeated the throne room. Everything under her reign was in its place, but I knew the only truth was entropy. I allowed vines to grow along the walls, and I welcomed the chaos that came with life.

"It suits you. As twisted and gnarled as your black soul."

I couldn't help but laugh. "The Great Ozma, brave to the last. Do you not remember that I knew you as a child, as the frightened child named Iris who shook in her boots?"

"I remember you were a friend to my family and my kind, before you sold your soul to your cruel goddess."

"She is only cruel to those who deny her. For those that worship her, she is kind."

Ozma snapped her head in my direction and looked at me in the eyes. "Hera has never been kind to anyone. She has only been polite to anyone who carried out her will."

Ozma was no longer the frightened child I had known, or the naïve one that took the throne. She had grown into a formidable force behind her still child-like appearance.

"Come, Ozma," I said, raising my arm into the air. "We have an adoring public to meet."

Slowly, Ozma rose into the air with the will of my magic. I strolled across the black velvet carpet that connected my throne to the terrace outside of the throne room, as she trailed in the air behind me.

I had demanded my loyal nobles summon Oz's denizens to the Green Keep for a demonstration of my power. I would kill Ozma in front of them, and then all who denied my right to rule would know that I am the true queen of the Dream Realm. I peered down from the balcony and saw the courtyard filled with thousands of my subjects, gathered in a mass like the sea.

"My people," I said with a smile. "I have brought you here to witness a historic moment in our great city." I pushed my hand outward, and Ozma floated into the air above the crowd. There was a collective gasp. Some pleaded with me to spare their queen, but most fell silent, as if they finally conceded the failure of their rebellion. "Many call Ozma the rightful heir, but I call her my prisoner. You say she is all powerful, but look at her now, dangling in the wind, a helpless nothing."

"Please," Ozma said. "Don't."

"Finally, a little respect from you," I shouted. "Too little too late." I raised both hands high into the air. "See the penalty for treason!"

I brought both my hands in front of me and clapped them together. Ozma kicked for a moment in mid-air and met my eyes. There was an innocence in her face, a pleading that was delicious to behold. Then, she plummeted to the ground and crashed upon the cement in my courtyard, bursting into a cloud of dust.

"I am the only power in Oz now. Fall behind my rule or join Ozma in oblivion."

The crowd watched me silently as I spun on my heel and walked back into the castle. The large wooden doors closed behind me, and I could barely contain my excitement. Finally, the brat was dead, and I could focus on leaving this accursed continent for good.

CHAPTER 60
RED

"NO!"

My queen. My queen. I watched her tumble down to the ground from the royal balcony. I watched Nimue drop her like she was a piece of garbage and not the rightful ruler of Urgu.

I pushed myself through the crowd to the spot where Ozma had fallen, but I was too late. Her essence was floating into the air; nothing but a small pile of gray dust remained on the ground to commemorate my queen.

"Hey!" A hand grabbed my shoulder. I turned, ready to kill whoever was touching me. It was Balor. "We can't kill the Wicked Witch from here. We have to get up there to do it, and only you know the way."

He was right. He was always right. I wanted to linger and mourn for my beloved queen, but there was too much to do. We pushed back into the crowd and caught up with Chelle.

"This way."

The Wicked Witch thought the crowd would be stunned into silence, and eventually submission, after witnessing the execution of their queen, but the people of the Emerald City were not docile. They were as furious as I was, and their voices rose against the castle walls with hate and disdain for Nimue.

The crowd rushed the Wicked Witch's guards like waves crashing upon the sand and pushed through into the courtyard. The guards were too distracted by the crowd to notice us slip past them into the garden.

In the back of the garden rested a large bird feeder with the image of a peacock on it. It was Hypnos's peace offering to Hera, given after the first war between them when Urgu was first founded. He had placed the statue prominently in his favorite garden. It was a symbol of peace, but underneath rested a secret passage which led into a hallway next to the throne room.

"Hurry," I said. "This statue blocks the only tunnel into the castle. Push this."

Balor and I tried with all our might, but it wouldn't budge. The stone was heavy, but a century ago we moved it with little problem.

"You can't move it. The statue is magically enchanted," Chelle said. "I can smell it from here."

"Enchanted?" I roared. "Can you open it?"

Chelle looked up at the castle. "She's way more powerful than me. This is powerful and old magic. I wouldn't even know where to start."

"Try," I said. "Just try."

CHAPTER 61
CHELLE

I had a secret nobody knew about me.

I wasn't much good with magic. I had unlocked a spell here and a spell there, but aside from some shields and a slew of simple offensive spells, my knowledge of the arcane arts was limited. Breaking a complicated ward was well above my ability, especially one placed by the power of a god.

I couldn't tell that to Red, though. She would have insulted me, called me a coward. I had to give it a shot, for both of our sakes. Red was a dangerous person to have around when we were on the same side. I didn't want to see what happened if I crossed her.

I placed my hand on the ward. "*Aperi mihi debes.*"

Nothing happened. "*Nunc aperta.*"

Again, nothing. "*Get iam aperta!*"

Breaking wards was all about knowing the original spell and reversing it precisely. If you didn't know the exact incantation, then all your words were useless. If you didn't have the will to cast such a spell, then you would likely be dead before you even broke the first layer of the ward.

"Why isn't it working?" Red snarled.

"I don't know. I told you this was powerful and old magic. Something I have never seen before." I slapped my hand against the stone peacock. "This is not my area of expertise."

"What is your area of expertise?"

"Blowing things up."

"Then try that."

Could it be that easy? Could I just blow up the peacock and grant us to access the tunnel underneath the city? It wasn't that far-fetched. Powerful wizards often thought of the most complex spells they could conjure and made wards to protect against them. They overlooked preventing the easiest spells.

"It's going to attract a lot of attention."

"Then it had better work."

I shook my head, doubting myself, but offensive magic was something I knew pretty well. It was about the only thing I knew well. I knew how to fight, and that knowledge might be exactly what we needed to break Nimue's spell.

With my hands placed in the air before me, I whispered, "*Globulus igneus.*"

The fire grew in my hands and as I pulled them apart, it grew larger than my head. By the time I stopped its growth it was nearly the size of my body.

"I'd step back if I were you."

Red and Balor moved behind me. I pushed the fireball forward and it exploded on the peacock, sending it smashing into a thousand pieces.

"*Scutum caeli!*" I shouted and the air formed a shield around Balor, Red, and I until the debris cleared. Once it had, there was a hole in the ground where the statue once stood.

"Wow," Balor said. "I can't believe that worked."

"Stop!" We heard from the other side of the garden. I turned to see a dozen or more troops funneling inside.

"Go!" Balor shouted. "I'll hold them off and buy you some time!"

"But—"

"Go!" Balor insisted. "I'll be right behind you."

I grabbed Red by the cloak and pulled her toward the secret tunnel. She jumped inside and I followed, wishing Balor the gods' speed but knowing I would likely never see him again.

CHAPTER 62
ROSE

There was nothing to do in the dark cell except sit alone with my thoughts, and I hated them as much as I hated myself, and the position I'd put myself in by being gullible and naïve.

My thoughts had never been nice and polite, especially to me. They made me feel horrible things, so long ago I decided to fill my life with mundane tasks as often as possible to drown out the voices telling me to do terrible things to myself.

"You are worthless."

"You are pathetic."

"You are weak."

The longer I remained alone in the dark, the more my thoughts bombarded me with their negativity. I pulled my legs closer to my face and rested my head on them. I took a deep breath to calm my mind, but the minute I exhaled, the flood of my past transgressions crashed upon me.

"You will get Chelle killed trying to save you."

"The queen will die."

"Your body is already dead."

That might be true, but the thing was, even after everything that happened, and the fact I was probably going to die, my travels in Urgu had been the absolute best time of my entire life. I didn't have to worry about insulin, or money, or anything. I was just able to live in the moment.

That sounded weird, given that I came near to being fried by pixies, eaten by dragons, and drowned in the Cursed Sea, but it was still true. For the first time in my life, I actually had agency. I could influence things instead of having stuff just happen to me. I didn't know if I could go back to my mundane, painful life, where I had to beg for scraps.

Perhaps it was better that I died. Then, I could never return to Earth again.

"Now, don't think like that," I heard in the darkness. "This place is not worth a beauty such as yours."

I stiffened. "Who's there?"

Two bright purple eyes appeared in the darkness. "Do you not recognize me, child? Before I was imprisoned here, every human knew my name and feared whispering it out loud."

"Hera."

"Brave girl. Brave. It's a pity what must be done to you."

"Nothing has to be done. Whatever you're going to do, you're doing it because—well, I'm still kind of fuzzy on the whole reason why, actually, but I know it's you who wants to do something crappy to Urgu."

"It's not my fault," Hera said. "I wasn't imprisoned here by my own free will. I just want to get back to Earth, and the universe at large. Anything else is collateral damage."

"You're not going to get away with this."

"And who's going to stop me? The other gods agree with me. Their imprisonment in Urgu has always been unfair and unjust. Zeus and his ilk had no right to force us here. Returning to the universe is our birthright. Being cast out, our tragedy."

"They're not the ones about to destroy the Dream Realm. You are."

"That's because the others don't have the stones to endanger humanity. They fear the wrath of Zeus. I have no such fear. He will burn for his betrayal."

"And your vengeance is worth all our deaths, huh?"

There was a long silence. "Yes."

"At least you're honest. Not that that's any comfort."

"It might be, in the end."

The door opened and two guards entered. I looked at them, resigned to my fate, then back at the eyes, but they were gone. Part of me wondered if they were ever there to begin with.

CHAPTER 63
RED

I pressed my hand against the dank brick wall as we walked in the darkness of the passageway. The secret tunnel led under the castle and into the inner chamber nearest the throne room.

"Why didn't you do this before?" Chelle asked behind me.

"Excuse me?"

"If you knew about this passage, why didn't you use it before? You could have snuck in and taken out the Wicked Witch years ago."

"Ozma forbade it. She said that an assassination was not the will of the people and made us no better than The Wicked Witch."

"Even after everything she's done to Urgu?"

"Ozma believed that the death of the queen would create civil war and chaos, and that having a monarch was better than having the realm devolve into roving bands of thugs. And, if the other five kingdoms saw us as weak, they would attack."

Chelle scoffed. "That's stupid."

I couldn't argue with the gorgon. I wanted to kill the false queen and could have on at least a dozen occasions, but that wasn't the way Ozma wanted to regain her power. She believed only the will of the people could sweep her back into her rightful place on the throne. Now, those people were sweeping her up.

"Monarchs are weird."

"Tell me about it."

I finally reached the end of the passageway. Light streamed under the wall from the other side of the corridor. I knelt and listened. When I didn't hear anything, I pushed open the door and crept into the hallway.

"Usually this hallway is crawling with guards, but they must all be distracted with the mob brewing outside."

Chelle grinned. "Or the explosion that we caused."

"Or the explosion."

I pushed on the wall and it opened for me. On its other side was a painting of Hypnos, clad in black and surrounded by a black mist. When Ozma ruled Oz, the castle was full of reds, blues, and greens, cheery and happy. Now, everything from the roses that adorned the hallways to the tapestries were dark and gloomy.

"The throne room is on the other side of this wall," I said, pointing to the wall opposite the secret passage. "Be prepared to attack immediately. The queen will take no prisoners. We only have one chance to end her."

When we reached the entrance to the throne room, I heard the crescendo of a pair of feet running in our direction. I pushed Chelle back and watched as the Wicked Witch turned the corner and rushed down the hallway. I pulled out my daggers and leapt at her.

"Fool," the witch spat.

She spun around and faced me, slowly closing her fist. As she did so, my throat closed as well. I choked, trying to gasp for air.

"Did you not think I knew exactly what would happen if I killed your precious Ozma? That you would come here to seek revenge?" Her eyes darted to Chelle. "Without killing the child queen, I would never have found you again, gorgon. And I desperately need you if I'm going to leave this accursed place. There's a very good chance your spoiled girlfriend's soul doesn't work to destroy the veil between Earth and Urgu."

Her eyes flicked back to me. "You, I don't need at all."

She flung me against the nearest wall. My head smashed against the bricks, hard. I heard a sickening crack, and I fell to the ground. The last thing I saw before I slipped into unconsciousness was the Wicked Witch moseying toward Chelle. There was nothing I could do about it.

I had failed.

CHAPTER 64
CHELLE

"Stay away from me!" I shouted as the Wicked Witch sauntered toward me.

She smiled, revealing her perfect white teeth. "I don't think so. You're an absolutely essential component to my backup plans should the prophesy fall apart." She leaned in slightly and spoke in a stage whisper. "To tell you the truth, I don't think your beloved is the chosen one after all."

"No?" I asked.

Nimue shook her head. "I think it's you."

"Me?"

"You entered Urgu on the same day as the dreamer, and with a body, which is much more unique than some dull dreamer girl who we've seen a thousand times before."

"Then why are you killing her?"

Nimue shrugged. "The Red Rider seemed very convinced the dreamer was the key, and my master agreed with her. I hope they are right. At least then her death will mean something. However, it's no concern of mine if she is not the one. Her death is inconsequential. What's one more life after I have taken so many?"

"That's sick. What kind of person thinks like that?" I said, scooting back through the open archway and into the throne room. "You're toying with me, aren't you?"

"Of course I am. I so rarely have a day as entertaining as this one. I have defeated Ozma, the Red Rider, and found a way out of Urgu. Two ways, in fact. I could not be happier with how deliciously this day has played out. I honestly don't think I could take another bite."

I tried to move my arms to attack, but Nimue had locked them to my sides. I tried to kick free, but they were glued to the ground.

"I'll never help you," I said to her.

"You don't have a choice."

She was right. I didn't have a choice. All I had was the silly idea that somehow, I wouldn't die, and that idea was quickly fading further from reality. My life was very much in danger, and so was Rose's. I cared little about my own life, but a great deal about hers.

Something moved in my peripheral vision. From behind Nimue, I saw Red push to her feet. She came toward us, wanting to help, but I shook my head slightly. I didn't care about me. She needed to save Rose. As long as Rose was alive, I was safe. Even if I died saving her, my sacrifice would be worth it.

CHAPTER 65
ROSE

Another egghead scientist strapped a probe to my head, just like they had done in the pixie castle. The only difference was that this egghead scientist was a human and not a pixie. His face was pale, and his fingers were so long that they wrapped completely around my arm when he pulled my straps tight.

It had become an all too disturbing trend in my life to be the subject of somebody's experiment. Perhaps that was what Chelle meant when she said that it sucked being the chosen one.

"This isn't going to hurt one bit," the scientist said. He had dandruff flakes in his bushy mustache and thick glasses hidden behind safety goggles.

"You're lying," I replied. There was a time when I would have believed that lie, but those days were gone. "I don't like liars."

"Correct. I'm sorry. I forgot that you've been through this before. Nobody has ever escaped the machine except for you."

"Just don't lie to me. If you're going to kill me, get on with it."

"Sorry. I've always found that lying eases the minds of the subjects in their last moments. Do you mind if I ask how you survived your last encounter with the machine?"

"I grew about fifty feet in the air. Or at least my girlfriend did. To save me."

"Ah," the scientist said, as if that were a completely normal answer. "Well, that would do it. Then yes, this will hurt quite a bit."

"Why are you helping the Wicked Witch?"

"She promised I could go home if I did. She promised we could all go home."

"Did she tell you what you'd lose in the process? That all of Urgu will go up in smoke? That dreams would disappear? That all of humanity would go crazy because they could never dream again? Did she tell you all of that?"

"Yes, she did. And I agreed to help her. There are always problems to be had when making breakthroughs, but the positives outweigh the negatives. Can you imagine it? People from Urgu returning to Earth after hundreds of years away...what will happen to us? Can we survive without bodies? It's all so fascinating. We'll never know. Or should I say, I hope we'll know soon?"

"I don't like you."

The scientist smiled. "You don't have to. I don't like you, either. I nothing you. That is the prerogative of a good scientist. I take no pleasure or pain in what will happen. You are simply the means to an end. Now, open your mouth."

I didn't fight him. There was no point. I was already doomed. I opened my mouth and let him position the leather bit.

"Good. It will help to bite down on that, unless you want to lose your tongue."

Lose my tongue? I was about to lose my life. What did I care about my tongue? Still, I bit hard on the chomp, taking out all my frustrations on it. The scientist walked over to his computer terminal and grabbed the switch.

"Any last words?" He looked at me. "Oh, of course not, you have a gag in your mouth. Goodbye, then. Keep your fingers crossed this works."

I was not going to do that. I wasn't going to make it easier. I wanted my death to be a struggle, to mean something. I loved life, and I wasn't going to give it up without a fight.

When he pulled the switch, I closed my eyes and took a deep breath. The electricity flowed through my body, and a weird calm came over me.

I opened my eyes and found I was no longer confined to the bed. Instead, I floated above it. I saw myself being electrocuted on the bed —in excruciating pain, but I wasn't there to experience it. I was having an out of body experience, without the body. An out of soul experience.

I looked up to the ceiling and that's when I shot into the sky like a rocket ship. I broke through the ceiling, and through the next floor, and the next, until I was up above the castle and floating into the sky. Down below, hundreds of people fought in the streets, trying to force their way into the castle.

But I didn't stop there. I continued to rise at a hundred feet a second or more. When I finally stopped, I was high in the atmosphere above Urgu. I could see the whole continent wrap around a huge sea of water. It almost had the shape of Australia or a kidney bean, but the concave part was on the top instead of the bottom.

Though, I guess there is no top or bottom in the world, is there?

"No, there isn't," I heard behind me.

"Who said that? I am so sick of people doing that to me!" I turned around. This time, instead of two purple eyes, I saw a tall, statuesque man. His eyes were dark, and his black cloak fell in tatters around his shoulders, barely covering his arms and legs. His skin was darker than Chelle's and yet it glowed brightly as he moved toward me, shimmering in the darkness of the sky.

"I wish we had more time."

"Are you him? Are you Hypnos?"

He nodded. "I am he who bestows a blessing on one to lead my people, and that blessing falls to you, if you accept it."

"What are my choices? Accept your blessing or die?"

He nodded again. "Precisely. I wish there was a better choice...for both of us."

"Aren't you a god? Can't you make one?"

Hypnos shook his head sadly. "Even I have my limits. If I could make one, I would."

"I don't want this."

Hypnos stared blankly off into the distance for a long moment. "Most don't. Unfortunately, 'want' has very little to do with it."

I looked down at Urgu, hundreds of miles underneath me. "Seems like it should."

"Maybe, but unfortunately, your desire is beside the point. You are left with a difficult choice. Accept my blessing and live or deny it and vanish into nothingness."

I gulped. "Will it hurt?"

"Not much, and then nothing will ever hurt again. Nothing will ever anything again."

I sighed. "And I'll never see Chelle again, right?"

"You might, still, but it's uncertain. If you accept, then you certainly will."

I nodded firmly. "Then I accept, but before I do, tell me. What happened to you?"

He smiled. "In time you will find me. You will both find me."

"Both?"

Hypnos touched my forehead. A warm current flowed through me, and suddenly I snapped back into the room where I was strapped down and being electrocuted. The entire room was awash in sparks and electricity. But the electricity wasn't coming from the computer terminal. It was coming from me.

My hands shook so fast I could barely recognize them. I pulled them toward me, and the straps holding me down snapped like thin twigs. I kicked my legs and they broke free as well. In one motion, I hopped off the chair and placed my hand on the computer terminal. Sparks flew from it in every direction before it caught on fire. The scientist stared on in horror.

"Please," he whispered.

"Sleep."

The scientist fell to the ground without another movement. I walked to the door. It was a huge, metal thing, but when I placed my hand on it, it flew off its hinges. The guards in the hall drew their swords, so I placed my hands in the air and electrocuted them until they fell as ash on the ground.

I didn't know how I was controlling my power. I was barely thinking anything and yet I was able to wield great magic. I didn't know where I was going, and it didn't matter. Somehow my body moved me along toward an unknown target.

"Rose!" Red shouted. She stumbled down the hall. "What happened?"

I knew I wasn't going to hurt her like I had the others. I liked her. "Where is Chelle?"

"With the Wicked Witch." Red shook her head. "She's not doing good."

"Show me."

I floated behind Red through the corridors until we reached the throne room. Chelle was pinned under a tapestry on the far wall, struggling unsuccessfully to break free from the Wicked Witch's grasp.

"Leave her be!" I shouted. A bolt of lightning shot from my hand and electrocuted the witch. She shook violently and her body spasmed. I flung my hand sideways and the witch crashed through the wall and out onto the street.

The electricity inside me died down and I came to control my body and my senses again. I fell back to the ground. Red rushed over to me.

"Are you okay?"

I looked up at her. "I don't know," I gasped. "Help me to my feet."

She did, and I hobbled over to Chelle, who was lying dazed on the ground, her eyes unfocused. "Chelle?" I shook her lightly. "Chelle, get up."

Her eyes fluttered when she heard me, and she looked directly at me. "What? What happened? Rose, is that you?"

"Yes, it's me, and somehow I have powers now. I met Hypnos and I think he gave me his powers."

"So, it is true," I heard someone say.

I turned to Red. "What is true?"

She frowned. "I didn't say anything."

"He really is alive, isn't he?" I heard the voice again. It was familiar. "I thought my spell would have killed him. I wonder what happened to him, then."

Two purple eyes materialized in the darkness, and from that a cloud of black smoke billowed around them. Then shadows cascaded down to fill out her body, cloak, and head.

"Go away," I said, the power surging through my body again.

"Honey, you do not want to take on a god."

My eyes flashed with anger and electricity. The spark of Hypnos flowed through me. "No. You do not want to take on *me*."

"Scoff."

"Did you just say scoff?" I asked.

"I did, because it would have been too much effort to actually scoff. This game has grown stale. I don't suppose I can use you now anyway, so I will let you have your victory. But rest assured, I will find a way out of this hellhole if it's the last thing I do."

I clenched my fists and stood firm, even though I was scared stiff, or perhaps maybe because I was scared stiff. "If you touch us again, it will be the last thing you do."

Hera smiled. "I really do like you very much." She disappeared into a cloud of smoke which flew out the window and into the sky, vanishing from view.

"I don't understand any of what just happened," Chelle said, standing up shakily.

"Me either."

"I do," Red said. "With Ozma dead, Hypnos needed a new champion, a rightful heir, and he chose you."

"Me?" I said, meekly, barely able to believe. "But I'm just a nobody."

Red placed her hand on my shoulder. "So was Ozma. So were they all. Hypnos believed that only a nobody could lead without malice."

I nodded fervently. "Cool. Very cool." I cocked my head to one side. "That's cool, right? I think it's cool."

Red pulled her hand from my shoulder. "I think it's cool."

"I guess you got your wish, then," Chelle said after a long sigh, sadness dripping from her voice. "You're a somebody now."

I wrapped my arms around Chelle. "I've always been a somebody, because I've been a somebody to you."

"That is the corniest thing you've ever said," she said, and then she kissed me, long and deeply. I had only been kissed like it a couple times before, and always when Chelle was going on a trip. It was as if she was saying goodbye. I understood then, that she would not stay with me if I remained in the Dream Realm, and it broke my heart.

CHAPTER 66
CHELLE

"The Fates must entreat with a body should it come to them," Red said to me as we walked across the throne room. "That is their way. Therefore, you are the only one in Urgu who is guaranteed an audience with them."

I had conflicting feelings about seeking out the Fates. I wanted to return to Earth, but I didn't want to leave Rose. She was happy on Urgu, where I could never be happy. There were nice things about the Dream Realm, but I yearned to return home.

"Are you sure you won't stay with me?" Rose asked. The black door in front of us opened to the walkway to the Obsidian Spindle.

"I want to stay with you, but I can't," I replied. "Who knows what would happen if I stayed here with a body. The Wicked Witch could use it to leave Urgu. I'm a danger to the whole world if I stay here, including you. Maybe one day I will fall into a coma, or die in my sleep, and return the right way."

Rose smiled. "I would like that."

Light streamed into the throne room when Red opened the door to the bridge. Rose stood there and soaked it in. She was beautiful, and her newfound powers made her even more so. She sparkled like the light of a new day. She had found her place, and I had to accept that.

"Are you sure you won't come back with me?" I asked her. "Powers aren't so great, you know."

Rose shook her head, slowly and sadly. "Somebody needs to stay here and guard the realm against Nimue and Hera, and to find Hypnos. Once it was Ozma, and now it's me."

"This sucks," I said, walking out of the door.

"Totally."

Red joined us on the bridge. "When you reach the end of the bridge and come face to face with the hydra, only Hypnos's power can calm it. Do not wait, or it will strike."

Rose gave a curt nod. "I got it."

I wasn't so sure about her powers, but she was supremely confident, and I loved seeing her come into her own. She had been scared and meek on Earth, but here in Urgu, she was powerful and confident. Even though I didn't want to leave her, I did appreciate that she was at home in this land.

As we crossed the bridge, the terrifying hydra came into view. It had been resting behind a retaining wall but when we neared, it raised its seven serpent-like heads and let out a shriek. The Spindle stood behind it, but the great beast nearly blocked it completely from view.

I swallowed the lump in my throat and waited for Rose to step forward. She placed her hands in the air and closed her eyes. Her voice never wavered. "Sleep."

The hydras stared at her for a moment with its beady eyes, and then collapsed slowly on the ground one head after the other into a gentle slumber.

"It worked," Red said, with audible relief. "I had my doubts."

Rose smiled. "Me too."

We stepped over the hydra and made our way to the door of the

Obsidian Spindle. Rose looked at me. "This is the moment of truth. Place your hand on the door and tell it to open. With luck, it should open for you."

I placed my hand on the door. "Open."

But nothing happened. The door didn't budge. Again, I placed my hand on the door, and this time I closed my eyes. "Open."

Again nothing.

"Oh no," Rose said.

"What does it mean?" I asked.

"I think it means you can't go home."

I turned to Red. "Any ideas?"

She shrugged. "Ozma was the only person in Urgu who knew how the Obsidian Spindle worked, except for Hypnos. Until Rose can find him again, I have no idea what to do."

"I'm trying!" Rose said.

I placed my hand softly on her cheek. "I know you are."

I wanted to be upset, but I was in some ways relieved. I was compelled to go home, but I didn't want to leave Rose, and being forced to stay in Urgu meant I didn't have to make a choice. I could be with her and that was all I ever wanted, even if I couldn't be with her the way that I wanted.

"Don't worry," Red replied. "We will find a way. I swear it."

"Meanwhile," Rose said. "Looks like you have to stay here with me." She snapped her fingers, feigning frustration. "Drat."

I shook my head and closed my hand into hers. "I can think of worse fates."

And it was true. For all my posturing about wanting to go back home, all I really wanted was to be with Rose and to be happy. I couldn't be happy in Urgu, but I could be with Rose, and that was the next best thing. This was not what we intended, but anywhere we were together couldn't be so bad.

Maybe in time, I could convince her to come back with me as we worked to open the door to the Obsidian Spindle to change our fates.

Or maybe, our fates were already changed, and we just didn't know it yet.

You just finished *The Sleeping Beauty,* the first book in The Obsidian Spindle Saga. If you loved this book, please consider leaving a review on your favorite storefront. Reviews are the best way for me to see if people want me to continue a series.

THE WICKED WITCH PREVIEW

The Wicked Witch
Book 2 of the Obsidian Spindle Saga

By:
Russell Nohelty

Edited by:
Leah Lederman

Proofread by:
Katrina Roets

Cover by:
JV Arts

Formatting by:
Turbo Kitten Industries

This is a work of fiction. Similarities to real people, places, or events are entirely coincidental. *The Sleeping Beauty*. First edition. January 2021. Copyright © 2019 Russell Nohelty. Written by Russell Nohelty.

NIMUE

I'm cold.

I flew for the better part of the day and late into the following evening after being chased out of Oz by the whelp queen Rose. The wind stung against my face until I shook all over from the chill, but I dared not stop for even a moment until I reached Hera's keep far above the forests of the Dark Domain.

I could not risk traveling by foot for fear of being arrested. Even if my troops pledged fealty to me, I feared that their loyalties would now switch to the new queen. Teleporting would have brought me to Hera's castle more quickly; too quickly, actually. I had failed to keep her prize and feared her rash temper. I needed to give her a chance to cool down so she wouldn't pull me limb from limb the instant I showed up.

Ungrateful usurpers had no respect for what I'd built over the last century as the queen of Oz. I spent every waking hour in service to those ignorant hayseeds, and they had no appreciation for what I had done for them. Having my own subjects scream for my head was truly the end all of a rotten day.

The citizens of the Emerald City cheered my defeat as if I was a monster, and not their liberator. I would have brought them all with me back to Earth. We would have left the Dream Realm behind had I found a way through the Obsidian Spindle, but that wasn't enough for Ozma or her sycophants. Ozma had no vision, except to sow deceit. She turned the whole city against me. Her ilk turned Rose—the Dreamer—and the Gorgon against me, and now, I was a queen without a land to rule.

Hera gave me her blessing, but not control over her Dark Domain. Most gods of Urgu had no interest in ruling their kingdom, but Hera was a micromanager. She needed to bend every blade of grass to her will...and did not abide failure. In the hundreds of years I worked in her service, she killed many for less.

I don't even know how I failed. It all happened in a blur. One instant, my men were opening a portal back to Earth using the Dreamer's soul to power our machine. The power of the Dreamer was working. I could feel the veil between our worlds breaking apart, and then in the next instant, Hypnos gave his blessing to that silly little girl, and she cast me out of the castle.

I looked back at the Gates of Droangor, which separated Hypnos's land from Hera's and the other gods: the Sandlands, where Sekhmet's people roamed; the Mountains, where Agrona ruled; the Bogs of Insanity, where Loki kept council, and the Thatch, where Anansi kept his home.

In the distance, The Emerald City shone brightly over the Land of Oz, and behind it, the Obsidian Spindle stood tall, its gnarled black spire pointing high into the sky. It was there that the fates spun the destiny of men and protected the only door out of the Dream Realm back to Earth. One day that most precious resource would be in my control. I would unlock its secrets and find my way back to Earth. It was the only shred of hope I had left.

I looked across Hera's Dark Domain and saw her keep, high atop the tallest hill. It was there I had received Hera's blessing, and plotted to overthrow Ozma and rule the Land of Oz. Hera's palace was where I kept my library, filled with the forgotten knowledge of

Urgu. It was where I learned how to overthrow a queen and so I was returning so that I could plot my comeback.

The Land of Oz had hope now, in the Dreamer and her harem of misguided idealists. If I wasn't careful, that hope could spread throughout Urgu. Hypnos made sure of that when he adorned her with his blessing and brought his magic back to the world. For decades, his magic had faded from the Dream Realm, making my plans easier to enact. Now, I would require Hera's full force and support if I were to be successful. Somehow I would destroy Rose and her ilk once and for all.

To reach Hera's castle, it was necessary to climb a sheer rock face. She did not want visitors. Her subjects lived in constant fear of her, which made ruling her kingdom all the easier. She did not care if they lived or died. She only cared about one thing: escaping her prison and finally returning to the universe once again. Any other purpose was inconsequential, which is why we worked so well together.

Her castle was made from the same obsidian that forged the Spindle. Hera insisted on it, even though it meant the death of five thousand dwarves when they mined the ore from the deepest caves in Urgu and carried it up the mountain by hand. Obsidian was one of the few objects in the universe which could not be affected by magic. That was precisely what made the Obsidian Spindle impervious to my efforts to open it, and to Hera's repeated attempts to destroy it. When Hera made her own castle, she demanded the same level of invulnerability.

Even the Queen's castle in The Emerald City was not so impermeable as Hera's lair. Hypnos had created magical wards to bar Hera from coming and going as she pleased. During my reign I had disabled or reduced many of them to allow Hera and her shadow demons through my halls. Every piece of information about the wards was locked up in my library vault, and I killed anyone who knew anything about them, but I knew the Dreamer brat and her merry band would surely find a way to reinstate the protections against me and Hera.

I had to find a way back to the castle, and through the Obsidian Spindle, before the magical wards were raised again. Our retaliation must be swift and brutal.

The black shutters above Hera's throne room were open when I reached the castle. She knew I was coming.

Of course she knew that I was coming.

She was a god. There was not much in Urgu that she couldn't predict. Perhaps the last thing that truly surprised her was the return of Hypnos's power to the land, and how quickly the Dreamer used it to cast her out of the Emerald City.

The moment I flew through the windows they slammed closed behind me, and I fell to the ground, tumbling on the plush carpet in front of Hera's throne. Blue lights flickered along every wall, but otherwise the room was dark, which was how Hera wanted it. She could move freely through the shadows. In all my decades in her service, I had only seen her true form twice.

"You have failed me," Hera's stern voice boomed. Her violet eyes blinked in front of me, and that was all of her that I saw in the dark.

"I'm sorry, my queen. You must know that I tried my best. You couldn't expect me to know—"

"Silence!" Hera shouted. "I do not wish to hear your excuses."

"I'm sorry, your majesty."

"Yes," Hera replied with venom in her voice. "You are, aren't you? You are sorry for your existence."

I looked up, trying in vain to meet Hera's eyes. "You must know that I couldn't predict Hypnos coming back. Even you, in all your greatness, couldn't foresee that."

"Hrm."

I balled my fists up under me. "We were so close to victory, my queen. I believe that if we can simply retake the Emerald Ci—"

"There is no *simply* now, Nimue!" Hera roared. "Nothing is simple with the return of Hypnos. I told you to act quicker, but you chose to delay."

I bit the side of my lip, trying to control my anger at her accusation. She would not tolerate insolence, and my voice could not betray me. "It was not my choice. The pieces had to fall into place, and they had, your majesty. We were mere moments from glorious victory."

Hera sighed. "And yet, you ended up failing me in the most awful way possible. Not only did you fail to open a portal to Earth, but you also brought the magic of Hypnos back to this land. Unacceptable."

"Please," I begged. "Give me another chance."

"Why?"

I took a deep breath. *Project confidence.* "Because I am your best chance of getting back to Earth and you know it."

Her purple eyes blinked open and shot toward me. "If that is true, then there truly is no hope. Goodbye, Nimue. May your failures haunt you all your remaining days."

Before I could speak, Hera snapped her fingers and the blackness collapsed around me. I drifted away. The last thing I saw was a sly smile cracking through the darkness under Hera's eyes. She was savoring the moment of my banishment.

ROSE

"Ow!" I shouted as Chelle's blast singed my hand for the second time in the last hour. The throne room had become our makeshift training academy where we practiced magic between the stream of well-wishers waiting to kiss the ring of the new queen—me.

I hated the throne room. Every moment I spent there was an unwelcome one. Nimue, the despot queen who ruled before me, wanted to project an element of fear in any who entered and so she kept the place dark and menacing. Thick black tapestries blocked the light from the stained-glass windows behind the throne.

Since I took over the throne, at least, I had insisted the floor-to-ceiling windows leading to the balcony remain open at all times. I used them to look out upon the Emerald City, and the Land of Oz. Even in the rain, the breeze brought the warmth of nature into a castle that for too long had been cold and hollow.

I turned my face from the wind and gave Chelle an eyebrow. "Go easy on me, all right?"

She laughed. I loved her laugh, even when it was mocking me. "I'm sorry. It's just—you're so bad at this."

She was having a ball teaching me magic. For most of our relationship, she was the gorgon with incredible magical powers and I was just the normal by her side, but now we both had magic; I had recently been blessed by the god Hypnos himself and charged with carrying out his will on Urgu.

Unfortunately, Hypnos vanished into the ether before he could teach me how to use my powers. I could not find, or feel him, anywhere in Urgu. I had to rely on Chelle to teach me. It was not going well.

"I'm not bad. I just don't understand. You're telling me to speak a bunch of gibberish and then my powers will work, but they just keep...not working."

"You'll get it," Chelle replied, walking toward me.

I shook my head. "I doubt it. You're a terrible teacher."

Chelle picked up my singed hand and kissed it, the snakes on her head cooing sympathetically. "Better?" she asked.

"No," I chuckled. "Too bad you didn't learn any healing magic."

The snakes on her gorgon head flicked my arm with their forked tongues. Even little Albie, our old favorite snake who had lost a tooth, seemed happy, despite the fact that Chelle was miserable in Urgu and had been ever since we arrived a month ago.

We locked eyes for a moment, then Chelle said, "I just like smashing things too much to bother with healing."

I wrapped my arms around her and kissed her deeply. I could feel the sadness coursing through her. She hated Urgu. She wanted nothing more than to go back to Earth, but in the weeks since we'd banished the Wicked Witch, we hadn't gotten any closer to finding a way to open the Obsidian Spindle and speak with the fates. They were the only ones who could send us home.

Of course, I wasn't trying that hard to open the tower. I was perfectly happy as the Queen of Oz. Back on Earth, I was just a girl in a coma, a nothing burger from nowheresville; here in Urgu, I was one of the god-touched, and arguably the most powerful one, since my power came from the god of dreams, Hypnos, rightful ruler of the Dream Realm. Here, I had magic. Here, people looked up to me.

"Are you hungry?" I asked Chelle as she walked me back toward the gnarled black throne that Nimue vacated after we defeated her. In time, I hoped to learn how to bend the metal to my will, as she and Ozma had before me, but I hadn't been able to figure out the right spell yet. Chelle couldn't help because she was only skilled in offensive magic, not transfiguration.

If I didn't learn how to unlock my more powerful magic soon, then we risked another invasion, and my inevitable death at the hands of Nimue's formidable abilities. She'd had hundreds of years to develop her powers. I'd had a few weeks. I hated even more my lack of progress since that initial conflict. Part of me wished that Nimue would return, so I could feel the anger swell through me again like it did during my first encounter with her. I wondered if that would unlock something within me and give me control of the awesome power Hypnos had entrusted with me.

"Have you had any luck contacting him?" Chelle asked.

"No," I said, letting go of her hand and climbing the stairs to my throne. "Wherever he came from, he seemed to return there once he blessed me." I sat down. The metal laid uncomfortably beneath me, and the seat numbed my legs after only a couple of minutes. I hated the throne more than Chelle hated Urgu.

Unfortunately, I was stuck there sometimes eight hours a day, as people from all over the kingdom came to bend the knee and swear fealty to me. Their hollow platitudes were welcome, but they came from fear—fear of my power, which meant that I had to reflect power lest they realized I was unable to force their allegiance.

I had no interest in doing so. Fear might have worked for Nimue, but I had no desire to rule by it. Before Ozma disintegrated in a pile of dust, she told me that her goal for the kingdom was to bring equality to all her people, noble and peasant alike, and introduce technology into the world so they could move past their medieval era and into the industrial revolution and beyond.

I came from a world full of technology, and I could help the people move into the future. But I knew I wouldn't be able to do so if the denizens of Urgu feared me. I needed them to embrace the new world I planned to build. If they didn't, I would be deposed, like the nobles had deposed Ozma before me. I had to show them the way into the future was best for all of us.

The horns blew outside the throne room and I placed my head in my hands. "Christ. Can I get not one moment's peace?"

"What?" Chelle said with a smile. "You're popular. You're the Kristen Chenowith here, just like you wanted."

"I don't get it."

"When we get back to Earth, I'll take you to see *Wicked*. You'll love it. After this whole thing, it will probably even have a deeper meaning."

She insisted I was going back to Urgu with her, despite my constant objections to the contrary.

A young squire rushed into the throne room. His puffy black and green shirt was embossed with a peacock, the sign of Hera and sigil of the Wicked Witch. I hadn't had time to choose a new uniform, so they all wore the garb of Hera and Nimue. It made me uneasy every time I saw it.

"Your majesty, your majesty," The squire said in a thick cockney accent. "A guest comes to have an audience with you."

"Who is it?" I asked, sitting as straight and regally as possible.

"Your grace, she says she's Queen Aine, the fairy queen from the Enchanted Woods."

"The queen of the Unseelie? Here!" Chelle said, her hands glowing with flames. "Send her away before I blow her to bits."

"No!" I shouted. "That would cause an incident. She is one of my subjects, and I am obligated to speak with her. I might need her help in the days to come."

Chelle whipped around to face me. "You can't be serious."

I nodded. "As a heart attack. Show her in."

If you liked that preview, then pick up *The Wicked Witch* today.

Author's Note

I've had pieces of Urgu flash through my brain for the past decade, but it wasn't until 2018 that I was able to solidify it in a way that was satisfying to me...and more importantly, something that would be enjoyable for readers.

I've restarted and rewritten bits of this book dozens of times before it turned into its final form. I have a huge notebook full of stories and plans for the overarching series that I scribbled in for months before I started writing. Barely one percent of those ideas made it onto the page, but I wanted to flush everything out before I began so that I could seed ideas early on that will pay off many books later.

The world of Urgu is enormous and has a depth of scale unlike anything else I've ever written. Most of the time, I come up with things on the fly, and then reverse engineer how to jam them into their universe to make sense. This book was a welcome relief from my normal chaotic world building and allowed me to carefully mold the story.

Since I was a child, I have loved *Alice in Wonderland, The Wizard of Oz,* or any story that took characters to new and fantastical lands. I always dug movies like *Labyrinth* and places like Narnia. I would be lying if I said I still didn't want to get whisked away to a far-away land even now, in my late 30s.

I want to give special thanks to the *Dorothy Must Die* series. I have been battling with a structure for *The Obsidian Spindle Saga* a long time, and in that series, I found a way to construct these books and make Urgu come alive. If you know that series, you'll see a lot of parallels, especially in the way I built the ending.

Once you write a lot of books, you start to recognize the things you love writing about, even if you can't quite put your finger on why you keep coming back to them. I've written over twenty novels, and the threads that I kept pulling were fantastical worlds, magic, independent and willful female leads, demons, Hell, mythology, horror, death, loss, destiny, and fairy tales. This series is the "kitchen sink" series for me, in which I've poured everything I love.

The Sleeping Beauty was a joy to write but coming up with the plot and the characters took a lot of work. I knew some pieces though, even at the beginning:

- Somebody would fall into the Dream Realm.
- Her lover would need to come in to find her.
- They would have to make it to the Obsidian Spindle.
- Everything would be a play on fairy tales or mythology.
- There would be a Red Rider.

That was about it, more of a hodgepodge than a cogent narrative. Then, inspiration came from a most unlikely place. I was looking through my favorite cover designer's portfolio and came across the original cover for this book, which I bought before I ever wrote one word of this book. Literally exactly as it existed at release, except for the subtitle, "The Obsidian Spindle Saga." The girl asleep on a white background, black ooze seeping out of her...it perfectly encapsulates everything I wanted to do with the book. It is magical, and artful, and beautiful.

The cover gave me two things I desperately needed: a way to flip fairy tales on their heads in a dark and wonderful way, and a path into Urgu. I knew then that the book would be about a girl who went into a coma and fell into Urgu and had to wake herself up.

I came up with the part about the diabetic coma months later when I began to read about people who were dying because they couldn't afford their medication, and how some diabetics were paying as much as $750 a month for insulin.

I watched friends of mine use GoFundMe to raise money for their medication and cried when another of my acquaintances died because they couldn't raise the cash to pay for their insulin. I was horrified that anybody would have to scrounge and beg for their lives, and that became something I wanted—no, something I *needed* to talk about in this book series. It kept the character relatable and relevant, and added a tragic element to the love story between Rose and Chelle.

The heart of this story is the love between two tragic figures from different backgrounds. They love each other but can't be happy together because neither truly knows happiness except for where they find it in each other.

Rose finds a new sense of happiness in Urgu, but more because it allows her to escape her situation in life than because it was an idyllic place. Chelle knows that Urgu has even more problems than Earth, and her history with monster hunters and "chosen ones" means she can't stand by and watch the love of her life embrace such a bloody destiny.

There are so many threads left to pull. I hope you will stay with me to see how it all turns out for them, Urgu, and the battle between good and evil. If you like this, then you can join my mailing list at: www.russellnohelty.com/mail to get some free stories and be the first to learn when the next books drop.

Also by Russell Nohelty

The Obsidian Spindle Saga

The Godsverse Chronicles

Ichabod Jones: Monster Hunter

Cthulhu is Hard to Spell

My Father Didn't Kill Himself

Sorry for Existing

Gumshoes: The Case of Madison's Father

The Invasion Saga

The Vessel

Worst Thing in the Universe

The Void Calls Us Home

The Marked Ones

The Little Bird and the Little Worm

Gherkin Boy

Find a complete list at

https://www.russellnohelty.com/books/

About the Author

Russell Nohelty is a USA Today bestselling author, publisher, and speaker. He is the author of dozens of novels and graphic novels including The Godsverse Chronicles, The Obsidian Spindle Saga, and Ichabad Jones: Monster Hunter. He has a very entertaining newsletter, which you can join at www.russellnohelty.com. He lives in Los Angeles with his wife and dogs.

Get one of my favorite books for free at:
www.russellnohelty.com/mail
Substack:
https://authorstack.substack.com
Bookbub:
https://www.bookbub.com/profile/russell-nohelty

www.ingramcontent.com/pod-product-compliance
Lightning Source LLC
Chambersburg PA
CBHW050438200726

48295CB00024B/711